Jed Mercurio was a doctor before turning to writing. He created the TV comedy series *The Grimleys* and in 2002 the *Guardian* named him one of the five best début novelists of the year. *The Penguin Expedition* is his first work for children.

the PENGUIN Expedition

JED MERCURIO

illustrations by Jeffy James

WALKER BOOKS

AND SUBSIDIARIES

LONDON • BOSTON • SYDNEY • AUCKLAND

First published 2003 by Walker Books Ltd
87 Vauxhall Walk, London SE11 5HJ

2 4 6 8 10 9 7 5 3 1

Text © 2003 Jed Mercurio
Illustrations © 2003 Jeffy James

This book has been typeset in Sabon, Hotsy Totsy,
Highlander, John Handy and OPTI Opus

Printed and bound by Creative Print and Design (Wales), Ebbw Vale

British Library Cataloguing in Publication Data:
a catalogue record for this book is
available from the British Library

ISBN 0-7445-9092-2

www.walkerbooks.co.uk

To Baby E. & Molly Moo

For their valuable guidance and generous support,
the author thanks Tim Bevan, Eric Fellner,
Debra Hayward and Chris Clark
of Working Title Films.

Chapter One

At the bottom of the world lay the land of Antarctica. Snow-white wilderness stretched from one deep blue ocean to another. Antarctica was supposed to be the coldest place on Earth, but today the weather was hotter than ever. In the blue sky, the birds flew far and wide, squawking and looking for shade. In the sea, a whale swam up to gasp a jet of spray from its spout. The sun began to scorch its slick blue back. The whale flicked its tail and sank below the ice-cold water.

On top of a towering cliff of ice stood a penguin. His name was Scott, and he felt sad and scared. The ice was melting. All around, lumps were breaking off the cliffs and falling into the sea. Some were the size of houses. They crashed into the water, where they turned into icebergs. Scott raised a flipper to shield his eyes from the sun, and watched them float away. They glided to the horizon, then slipped over the edge of the world, and he knew that they would melt and never return.

A noise startled him. It was a rushing noise that got louder and louder. Scott's best friend, Humboldt, looked up at him through the thick spectacles that bridged his pointy beak.

"Scott, what's happening?" he asked.

The noise sounded like a fast-running river. Humboldt put his flippers over his earholes. Scott pointed at a big pipe sticking out of the cliff. A river of dirty brown sludge was pouring into the water below, turning the blue tranquil bay into a stinking bog.

What few fish there were coughed and spluttered, then, in panic, dived and scattered. But, before they could swim away, the water began to swirl. Another pipe opened, and began to suck them all in.

Over the deafening noise, Scott shouted, "The next Cycle's started! Come on, Humboldt, this is our chance!"

He scrambled over the ice towards the edge of the next cliff, with Humboldt scampering after him.

"Hurry!" Scott called.

"I'm waddling as fast as I can!" cried Humboldt.

They scurried alongside the big pipe which was sucking the fish out of the sea and carrying them towards a giant factory. The factory was built of ice. When Scott and Humboldt neared it, they saw that its walls were dripping as they melted in the sun. Stuck on the fence, a sign said:

```
BEAK CORPORATION
KEEP OUT!
```

Humboldt skidded to a halt. From inside the factory came the rumble of machines. "Why don't we just go home now?" he said. "It must be nearly time for tea."

Scott shook him by the beak. "What are you?" he said. "Penguin or chicken?"

Humboldt watched as Scott crawled under the fence and squeezed through a small gap where the pipe passed through the factory wall. Now he was alone. Squawking with annoyance, he crawled under the fence, slipped through the gap and plunged into the factory after Scott.

Inside, it was even hotter than it had been out in the sunshine. Humboldt's spectacles steamed up, so that he had to wipe them with his flippers. When he could see again, he registered that Scott was already crouching behind the big pipe.

Scott waved a flipper, saying, "Get down." Humboldt went and hid next to him, and together they peered over the top of the pipe into the factory.

Hundreds of penguins were working in an enormous chamber. Every one of them wore an overall with a patch that read BEAK CORPORATION in big letters. A few were scuttling from one large machine to the next, but most stood at their stations where, with their flippers, they pulled levers or pushed mushroom-shaped buttons.

Scott and Humboldt saw that the big pipe led to the largest machine of all, labelled THE HOMOGENIZER. It was pouring the fish into this machine. Gauges quivered, valves let out steam and it shook from side to side. Then, a few seconds later, from the bottom of the Homogenizer, tumbled lots and lots of little black cubes. They travelled along a conveyor belt and then dropped into tin cans. The workers were sealing the cans and labelling them BEAK'S FISHY DELIGHT.

"Yuck," whispered Scott. "That's the last time I eat Beak's Fishy Delight."

Humboldt said, "I kept telling my mum I could taste heads and eyes and fins, but she made me eat it just the same. Otherwise I got no pudding. Yesterday it was sardine ice-cream..."

Ignoring him, Scott pointed at a pipe that came out of the side of the large machine and soared high into the factory roof. Black fumes were hissing out of a valve, and all the workers nearby wore gas masks over their beaks. "There," he whispered, "that's what we're after. Come on."

Scott crawled to a metal ladder nearby and began to climb. He looked down at Humboldt, who was still crouched in terror behind the pipe. *"Come on,"* he said.

Trembling, Humboldt crept to the ladder, and then he too started to climb. "I'm scared of heights," he moaned. "Everything starts spinning. It's called 'vertigo'." His protests were to no avail. Scott was already halfway up the ladder.

At that moment, the Homogenizer began to quake. Its valves spluttered. Then, instead of firing cubes of Fishy Delight onto the conveyor belt, it coughed out a few small pellets and stopped.

A voice boomed out across the factory, "WHAT'S HAPPENING TO MY FISHY DELIGHT?"

From a lofty balcony, a pair of cruel eyes glared down at the hundreds of workers below. There was no mistaking the gigantic beak beneath those eyes, nor the huge cigar in that beak, nor the expensive waistcoat that stretched to cover the plump breast. "It's *him*," Scott whispered. "That's Boss Beak himself."

It was the first time Humboldt had ever heard fear in his best friend's voice. It sent him scampering up the ladder as fast as his flippers could carry him.

Boss Beak repeated, "WHAT'S HAPPENING TO MY FISHY DELIGHT?"

There was a whirring sound, followed by the squeak of rubber tyres across the ice floor. Boss Beak heaved himself round to look at his chief scientist. "Ah, Doctor Frost," he said.

Doctor Frost sat in a motorized wheelchair that he had designed himself. He wore a white laboratory coat and a monocle over one eye, and one of his flippers was mechanical. He was a great scientist, but sometimes his experiments resulted in explosions. "The fish supplies, sir," he said. "They are running low. Soon there will be no fish whatsoever in Penguinville Bay."

"Then build a bigger pipe," Boss Beak commanded. "Build a bigger pipe with a more powerful turbine that will suck up every fish in the ocean, and then, when there are no more fish left, build an even bigger pipe with an even more powerful turbine that will suck up every fish in the next ocean – on and on, Doctor Frost – on and on, until we have eaten every fish and plundered every ocean!"

"A bigger pipe. A more powerful turbine. Eat every fish. Plunder every ocean. Yes, sir, I shall begin my designs at once."

By now Scott and Humboldt had reached the top of the ladder. "Hold tight, Humboldt – I won't be long," said Scott.

He stepped out onto the roof of the factory. In one direction, all was the deepest blue. In the other, all was the brightest white. He could see the small town of Penguinville where all the penguins lived and, beyond it, a vast snowy wilderness. But above him, there was no sun or blue sky. A cloud of thick black fumes from the factory chimney hung overhead. Scott took out a small test tube and waited for the fumes to fill it.

Still at the top of the ladder, Humboldt was trying not to look down at the factory floor far far below, but he couldn't stop himself. The workers and the machines and the crates of Beak's Fishy Delight all started spinning. They spun faster and faster. "Scott," he groaned, "I'm feeling a bit queasy..."

The last wisp of black gas filled Scott's test tube and he sealed it with a rubber stopper. "I've got the sample," he reported, and climbed back onto the ladder. "If we get out now, we can—"

"Scott," said Humboldt, "I think I'm going to be sick."

"Hold tight, don't look down," Scott told him, "one step at a time."

Humboldt repeated, "Hold tight, don't look d—"

Then he *was* sick.

"Sorry, Scott."

"What happened?"

"I looked down."

Humboldt's vomit fell down and down, and plopped onto Boss Beak's head like a custardy hat.

Boss Beak wiped Humboldt's lunch from his head feathers. Then he looked up into the roof of the factory and saw the two boy penguins far above. His eyes burned with fury. "SECURITY!" he boomed.

The security chief, Rocky "Ice" Berg, stomped out onto the factory floor. He was not a tall penguin – in fact, he was quite short – but he was built like a barrel of fish oil.

"SEIZE THEM!" roared Boss Beak.

"Quick!" cried Scott. He grabbed Humboldt by the flipper and pulled him back out onto the factory roof.

From below came the sound of Ice clanging his way up the ladder after them.

"What now?" wailed Humboldt.

Scott pointed down at a vat of thick brown sludge.

"No way!" said Humboldt. "No way am I jumping into *that*!"

"The fall'll probably kill us anyway," said Scott. He grabbed Humboldt by the flipper and together they leapt off the roof, screaming and squawking as they fell.

They plunged into the warm dark sludge, which was draining out of the vat into a big pipe. Tumbling end over end, Scott and Humboldt were sucked into the pipe just as Ice clambered out onto the factory roof.

"DO YOU HAVE THEM YET?" Boss Beak yelled from below.

Ice scanned the roof but the boy penguins were nowhere to be seen. His only answer was a rough growl.

"Sir, they might have jumped," Doctor Frost suggested to Boss Beak. "Into the factory waste. They'll surely drown."

Far away, at the ice cliffs, the rushing noise started up again. It grew louder and louder until a river of sludge burst out of a large pipe and poured into the sea. In the sludge were two dark brown lumps the size of small penguins. The lumps hit the water and sank. A few seconds later, they rose to the surface. The sludge fell away, and the two "lumps" were revealed to be

Scott and Humboldt. Scott waved his test tube at Humboldt. Inside it, safely sealed from the sea water, was the factory chimney's black gas.

Chapter Two

The next morning, the sun rose on Penguinville, its light glinting on the ice panes of the shops and offices in the town centre. Out in the suburbs, igloos lined the snowy streets. In one of them, an ordinary penguin family was going about its morning routine. Amelia was in her nestroom. She was supposed to be getting ready for school. Instead, she was surfing the Internet with one flipper and texting a friend on her mobile phone with the other.

Outside the birds were singing. Amelia stepped to the ice window and saw gulls and petrels swooping through the air. She frowned. Penguins were birds, too. Amelia was a penguin. So why couldn't she fly? She climbed onto her nest and stood right on the edge. She held out her flippers and counted, "One, two, three..." and then jumped, flapping her flippers as fast as she could.

Downstairs in the kitchen, Amelia's mum and dad heard a loud crash.

"Amelia?" her dad called. "What's going on up there?"

"Darling?" added her mother. "You're going to be late for school. You're not waddling the Net again, are you?"

"She asked me if she could set up her own web site," muttered her father.

"Whatever would she do with a webbed site? Webbed *feet* – now for them I can see the use."

"Not *'webbed* site'," groaned Amelia's father, shaking his head. "It's—"

Amelia limped downstairs. She was rubbing her beak and her feathers were all ruffled. "Mum," she said, "aren't there *any* penguins who can fly?"

"Of course not, dear," her mother replied.

"But penguins are birds and birds can fly, so why can't we?"

"Always with the questions. Ask your father."

"Dad, penguins are birds and birds can fly, so why can't we? Why? Why?"

Her father was reading his newspaper. He didn't look up. "Ask your mother," he said. Then he wiped sweat from his brow. "I see the weather forecast predicts another hot day."

"But it's got to get cold again soon. Surely,

dear?" replied Amelia's mother, and instead of answering Amelia's question, they started an argument about the weather.

Amelia folded her flippers in disgust. "Grown-ups don't know anything," she muttered. "They talk as if they do but they don't."

Her mother gave Amelia her schoolbag, combed down her feathers and kissed her on the beak. "Off to school now, darling," she said.

A beeping sound came from Amelia's pocket. She took out her mobile phone and saw a text message from her friend: **cu @ bch!**

"If I'm late home, it's because I've gone to the beach," she said.

"Gone to the beach?" her father repeated. "Who said you could go to the beach?"

But Amelia had already scuttled out of the door. There were no clouds in the sky and the sun was burning brightly. Everywhere, ice was melting. It dripped off the roofs of all the igloos. Panting in the heat, grown-up penguins were trooping to work. They made a black-and-white line that pointed out of town towards the Beak Corporation factory. Already a black cloud loomed over its giant chimney stack.

The kids were all going to school. Amelia saw a crowd of them just a few steps ahead of her. In the crowd were Scott and Humboldt. "Hello, Scott. Hello, Humboldt," she called.

"Hello, Amelia," Scott called back.

He was always happy to see Amelia. He was too shy to tell her, but he thought she was the prettiest penguin in the whole school. She had big eyes and shiny feathers and her small beak had a cute upturn.

"What's happening?" she asked.

"They're taking the temperature with the town thermometer," Scott answered.

A giant thermometer stood in the middle of the crowd. Scott's father, Principal Flipper, the headteacher of Penguinville School, was staring at it in disbelief. "This morning's temperature," he announced, "is only five degrees below freezing!"

Everyone gasped.

"Well, no wonder we feel so hot!" cried Humboldt.

Principal Flipper cleared his gizzard. "Children of Penguinville," he began, "owing to this extremely bad weather, I hereby declare today a no-snow day!"

All the children cheered.

"Great," said Amelia. "Now we can go to the beach straight away!"

"But Scott," Humboldt protested, "this is the perfect chance to take more weather measurements."

"OK – well, see you," said Amelia, and set off

for the beach with her friends.

"No, wait!" Scott called. "Amelia, I'd love to come to the beach with you. I mean, I'd love to come to the beach. We can bring our equipment along."

"Great," said Amelia. "See you guys there."

Scott smiled. "Wow," he said to Humboldt. "I'm going to the beach – with Amelia."

Humboldt sulked. "I hate the beach," he moaned. "The other kids kick snow in my face. They twist my flippers behind my back and give me wedgies."

Scott patted his friend on the head. "For science to advance," he told him, "we all have to make sacrifices."

Chapter Three

The town of Penguinville was built on a gigantic piece of ice called an ice shelf. Where the edge of the ice shelf met the sea lay a flat area of snow the penguins called "the beach". The best strip of beach looked out on the tranquil waters of Penguinville Bay.

All the kids were starting up games of volleyball and water polo and ice hockey. Amelia heard the squawk of an albatross flying high in the sky, and looked up to watch it. Her eyes tracked the giant bird as it soared through the air. She leaned further and further back, tipping her head to follow it until, with a squawk of her own, she toppled backwards and splashed into the snow.

Amelia's friends giggled as she wiped snow from her eyes. When she looked up, a large figure was blocking the sun. Her friends stopped giggling and stared up, open-beaked. Amelia blinked to see who it was that was standing over her.

"Hi there," said the stranger. Then he reached down and, as if she were no heavier than a feather, lifted Amelia to her feet. The stranger was not much older than her, but he was twice her size and had the biggest muscles she'd ever seen on a penguin. He wore wrap-around sunglasses and a short-sleeved wetsuit, and carried a surfboard. His feathers were the blondest she'd ever seen.

"I'm the lifeguard," he said, and he smiled a brilliant white smile. "It's my job to watch over Penguinville Bay. Everyone calls me 'Dude'."

"Pleased to meet you, Dude," Amelia said. "I'm Amelia."

Dude continued, "Man, this heat is so uncool. I've got to chill out. Good meeting you, Amelia. Have a nice day." He winked at her and then strode to the lifeguard station, where he leaned his surfboard against the hut. With one flipper, he picked up a pair of binoculars and began to peer out to sea. With the other, he started curling a barbell.

Amelia's friends trilled, "But he's, he's ... *gorgeous*!" and they all giggled.

Only a little distance away, Scott and Humboldt were setting up their instruments.

Scott had watched Dude help Amelia to her feet, and he felt very jealous.

Just then, Humboldt swung the telescope and whacked him on the head. "Sorry, Scott," said Humboldt, "but I need some help here."

Scott stopped thinking about Amelia and helped Humboldt point their instruments at the sun. As well as the telescope, there was a special kind of mirror, and another instrument that was like a big camera. All of them had lots of pulleys, levers and lenses. Humboldt assembled them expertly, and then connected them to his portable PC.

Before they got to work, Humboldt smeared sunscreen all over his body. "I've got sensitive skin," he told Scott. "I burn easily." Then, together, they started taking measurements.

"The solar intensity is unprecedented," noted Humboldt. "Ultraviolet emissions are stronger than previously recorded."

"What does that mean?" said a voice.

Scott looked up in surprise. Amelia was standing right behind them. The boys had been so busy with their work, they hadn't even noticed her.

Humboldt began, "Solar emissions across the entire spectrum—"

Amelia frowned. Humboldt was the cleverest penguin in school; he was a genius. But sometimes it was hard to understand what he was saying.

"What he means," said Scott, "is that it's hotter than ever."

"And you need all this equipment to tell you that?" Amelia laughed. "Everyone knows how hot it is!"

"No, we're using these instruments to try and discover *why* it's so hot."

"You mean, you think something's *causing* it?"

"Yes," Scott replied. "Something *is* causing it, and we're going to be the first to find out what it is."

Before he could say any more, Dude's voice sang out across the beach, "EVERY PENGUIN OUTA THE WATER! EVERY PENGUIN OUTA THE WATER!"

Scanning the waves with his binoculars, Dude had seen dark shapes moving towards the beach.

"Leopard seals," he growled. Then he rang a bell and blew his whistle. All the penguins leapt out of the sea and scrambled up the beach squawking. Scott and Humboldt picked up their equipment and ran to safety. Amelia hurried to where her friends were sunbathing, and they picked up their towels and scampered to the lifeguard station. There Dude was running up a red flag over a sign that read:

BEWARE LEOPARD SEALS– NO SWIMMING WHEN RED FLAG IS FLYING

With no penguins left in the water, the dark shapes turned and swam away. Everyone looked at Dude and clapped their flippers and squawked their approval.

Amelia went up to him, "You're so cool! You saved our lives!"

Dude put his binoculars down and his sunglasses back on. He smiled his brilliant white smile and said, "Pumpin' iron, savin' lives – all in a day's work, babe."

"Seals are scary," she said.

"Man, they keep coming closer and closer to the beach," Dude mused.

"Why would that be?"

Dude shook his head. "Beats me, doll."

"Why do they want to eat us penguins when there are so many fish in the sea?"

"You know," he replied. "I don't see so many fish any more – it's kind of a big mystery where they've gone."

"It is," Amelia agreed. "Being a lifeguard is such an *important* job. How d'you cope with the responsibility?"

Dude smiled again and said, "Er…" He smiled a second time and said, "Er…" He couldn't think of anything to say. That happened to him a lot. He muttered, "Er … pumpin' iron, savin' lives – all in a day's work, babe." Then, feeling foolish, he shuffled away.

Amelia watched him go thinking that maybe *she'd* said something wrong. She decided not to let it worry her. She'd always thought Scott was the nicest kid in school, but he was nothing compared to Dude. Dude was the coolest penguin in Penguinville. Probably, she thought, Dude was the coolest penguin in the whole world. She smiled to herself and skipped back to join her friends.

Chapter Four

Just off the coast of Penguinville, a yacht sailed between the melting icebergs. The yacht was big and white and shiny, and on its side was written its name, *Q-Beak-2*. Though the hot sun beat down on its deck, the yacht's cooling system kept the swimming pool comfortably chilled.

Biff Beak – Boss Beak's son, and heir to the Beak fortune – broke the ice that had formed on the pool's surface and slipped into the water. "Brrr, freezing," he trilled. "That's better."

By the side of the pool, Biff's girlfriend, Brittany, lay on a deckchair. She was sipping a drink while one servant clipped her flippernails, and another styled her head feathers, and yet another used a fire extinguisher to blast her with cold air.

"Oh, darling," Brittany called to Biff, "if we don't eat soon, I fear I shall faint."

Biff climbed out of the pool and, before drying himself with a fluffy white towel, clicked a flipper at yet another servant.

The servant bowed to Brittany, "Ma'am, how might I be of assistance?"

"I want lobster," she replied.

"I regret to inform madam that we are out of lobster."

Brittany threw down her drink in disgust. "But I wanted lobster *so!*"

Biff sighed. "Leave this to me, darling. One simply can't get the staff these days." He marched across the deck and snatched the captain's binoculars out of his flippers. As his gaze swept across the sea to the beach of frolicking penguins and back again, something caught his eye. He twiddled the wheel to adjust the binoculars' focus. Set back from the beach was a little café. Normally, it was shut on weekdays, but Biff could see lines of penguins queuing for food and cold drinks.

"Skipper," ordered Biff, "set course for Penguinville Beach Café!"

"Aye aye, sir!" the captain replied.

By the time the yacht sailed into port, Biff had dressed in a blue yachting blazer with shiny gold buttons. He led Brittany across the jetty to the Beach Café. Steam rose from the kitchen and part of the café was melting in the sunshine. The café manager was calling out orders to his wife, the cook.

"One fish royale," he called, "a double fish-burger and fries, fish surprise, one fish club with extra fish and a side order of fish."

The cook shouted back, "Colin, how many times do I have to tell you it's melting in here?"

"Who cares," answered the manager, "when business is this good?"

Biff and Brittany looked around, wondering why the café was so busy. They both had private tutors, so they didn't know that Principal Flipper had let everyone off school today.

Scott and Humboldt were sitting at the only table in the shade. Humboldt had insisted, because the sun brought out his eczema. While he studied pages of scientific data, Scott went to the serving hatch to collect their lunch.

"My word," Biff complained, "this place is so full of riff-raff that we'll probably catch psittacosis."

Just then, the café manager saw Biff and Brittany. At once, he scuttled over and bowed. "Mister Biff," he said, "welcome to the Antarctic Riviera! And your girlfriend, Brittany – what an honour!"

"Your fish – now it is fresh fish, isn't it?" Brittany asked. "I simply can't bear it if it's not."

The manager hesitated for a moment, looking

uncomfortable, but then turned on a big smile. "But of course," he lied. "Just this morning I caught them myself in Penguinville Bay, and my wife has cooked them using only the freshest ingredients."

In the kitchen, the cook hurriedly pushed a big barrel of Fishy Delight into a cupboard where no one could see it. Her husband had gone fishing every morning this week but he hadn't caught a thing. So they'd been forced to buy a wholesale supply of Fishy Delight from Boss Beak and use that instead. She had worked wonders turning the horrible paste of fishy parts into a series of tasty dishes.

Boss Beak, who charged the highest prices, was delighted when yet another independent trader had been forced to turn to him for supplies. He wanted to own everyone and everything in Penguinville and, with the fish shortage, it looked like he'd succeed.

"Excellent," Biff told the manager. "We'll have this table."

Biff was pointing at Humboldt's table. Without a second's hesitation, the café manager tipped Humboldt out of his chair onto the floor and swept away his pages of data. "Our best table – for you, Mister Biff and Miss Brittany," he said.

Humboldt picked up his pages and moved to

another seat. He wanted to say something, but he was too scared of Biff's father. Now that he was sitting in the full glare of the sun, his face started to turn red.

Biff laughed. "Hey, geek, I hope we can tell the difference between your face and our lobster."

Scott returned from the serving hatch with a tray of food. "Leave him alone, Biff," he said. "You're nothing special just 'cause your dad owns most of Penguinville."

No one ever answered back to Biff. He was so shocked that he couldn't think of anything to say, so he turned away and ignored Scott's remark.

An old penguin staggered into the café. He had a face like leather and his feathers were falling out. He was drinking from a bottle wrapped in a brown paper bag. He looked at what everyone was eating and slurred, "In my day, a penguin was a penguin. You ate your fish raw, with the head *on*."

Then the old penguin spotted Scott. "I am the great Henson," he declared. "I was the last penguin to see your grandfather, Shackleton Flipper. I saw him on the day he set out for Base Camp Albatross, before he was lost in the blizzard to end all blizzards!"

Scott cringed. Whenever Henson saw him, he

32

always told this story.

"This is the expedition, the day we set out," Henson went on, showing Scott a fading black-and-white photograph of a dozen penguins, some standing, some seated, grouped together for the camera. Scott had seen the photograph many times before.

Next Henson showed him a black-and-white picture, just as faded, of a bearded penguin wearing hobnailed boots, tweeds and seal furs. "I took the last ever picture of the great Shackleton Flipper," he said, and then he started to sob. "If only I'd stayed with him, if only…"

Biff called, "Change the record, Henson. We've heard this hogwash a million times."

At the commotion, the café manager waddled into action. "We don't serve your kind!" he snapped at Henson.

"No," shouted the cook, "we only serve fish!" and everyone laughed.

The manager bundled Henson out of the café and onto the beach where he staggered around in the snow until eventually he collapsed in a heap. Then he drank some more from his bottle and soon he was fast asleep.

Biff looked at Scott and sniggered. "Just when you thought you'd got the better of me, the town drunk showed up to remind everyone that your grandfather is the biggest joke in the history of very big jokes."

Scott shook. He always got upset when anyone teased him about his grandpa. "Nobody knows for sure," he said. "He *could've* reached the South Pole. I don't care what anybody says, Shackleton Flipper was the greatest explorer in penguin history and one day I'm going to be just like him!"

Now everybody was laughing. Scott was too embarrassed to stay. He leapt to his feet and ran out of the café.

"Scott, wait!" Humboldt called. He gathered up the pages of scientific data as fast as he could and scampered after his friend.

But, unnoticed by Humboldt, one of the pieces of paper had fallen to the ground. Biff picked it up.

Brittany sighed. "Biff, please don't tell me you've got the science bug too."

Biff studied the piece of paper. It had a lot of numbers printed on it that he didn't understand, but at the top of the page was written:

BEAK CORPORATION POLLUTION DATA

"Hmm," he said, scratching his beak. "Maybe I have."

Chapter Five

The next day was no colder. In fact, according to Humboldt's calculations, it was the hottest so far. The sun shone in a bright blue sky. Icicles dripped from the roofs of igloos. The streets of Penguinville were turning to slush.

Once again, Principal Flipper had closed the school so all the kids were down at the beach. Most were playing ice hockey, though they had to take frequent breaks for cold drinks. Some, who had been out in the sun too long, had sunburnt heads and beaks. Amelia and her friends put up umbrellas to give them shade. Dude patrolled the beach, staring out to sea with his binoculars and spinning his surfboard in the snow.

Scott and Humboldt were operating their scientific equipment. Scott pulled a lever to adjust a lens, while Humboldt took measurements.

Then he used the measurements to draw a graph.

After about an hour, Amelia picked up her towel and told her friends she was going to watch the icebergs float out to sea. None of them wanted to come, so she climbed up the ice cliff by herself.

Down on the beach, Scott made another adjustment to the lens. Humboldt took a reading and plotted the number on his graph.

He blinked at the graph. The pencil dropped from his flipper.

"What's wrong?" asked Scott. "Humboldt?"

Humboldt was so excited he started to wheeze. He had to take a gasp from his inhaler. "It's ... it's..."

"It's what?"

"Scott," Humboldt announced at last, "it's the answer."

Just then, Amelia's voice squawked out over Penguinville Bay, *"I'M THE QUEEN OF THE CASTLE, AND YOU'RE THE DIRTY RASCALS!"*

Scott and Humboldt peered up to see her perched at the very edge of the ice cliff.

"This heat could make the ice give way at any second," Humboldt warned.

"AMELIA, BE CAREFUL!" Scott shouted. "STEP BACK FROM THE EDGE!"

"SILLY!" Amelia shouted back. "NOTHING'S GOING TO HAP—!"

The ice beneath her feet shuddered. A piece the size of a car broke off and plunged into the sea. Amelia squawked in terror.

"HANG ON!" shouted Scott. "I'M COMING!"

Every penguin on the beach stopped what he or she was doing. They watched Scott climb towards Amelia. As the ice crumbled under her, she clung on by her flippertips.

"AMELIA, HANG ON!" Scott called out.

From the lifeguard station, Dude saw black shapes swimming underwater towards the bottom of the cliff. "Leopard seals," he growled, sliding down his ladder, dragging his surfboard behind him. He threw the board into the water, jumped on, and paddled as hard as he could with his muscle-bound flippers.

The leopard seals reached the bottom of the cliff and came up out of the water. When Amelia saw them, she screamed. They were ten times the size of a penguin, with razor-sharp teeth, and they were roaring up at her.

"HELP ME! HELP ME!" she shrieked.

"HOLD ON!" cried Scott. "I'M NEARLY THERE!"

Just before Scott could reach her, the ice broke and Amelia lost her grip. She flapped her flippers, trying to fly. She flapped and flapped and, for a moment, believed she was hovering.

"I'm flying!" she cried.

But of course she wasn't, because penguins can't fly, and she fell, squawking and shrieking into the water. The leopard seals swam towards her.

Dude stood on his surfboard and caught a wave. He surfed towards Amelia at record speed. A seal snapped its jaws but, before it could do anything more, Dude scooped Amelia up by her flipper and plonked her on the back of his surfboard. "Hold tight, babe," he said.

He turned the board back towards the beach, and, with Amelia gripping his legs, they started to ride a wave home.

The penguins watching from the water's edge, called out to Dude to hurry – a leopard seal was catching up with the surfboard. Dude leaned to the left and then to the right, throwing up sprays of water, but the seal followed. It got close and took a bite out of the back of the board. Dude wobbled but Amelia held tight and they got their balance back. Dude steered them towards an iceberg.

"Watch out!" shrieked Amelia.

"Hold tight, babe," said Dude.

He kicked up the front of the board and they jumped up onto the iceberg, which sloped upward like a ramp. Dude and Amelia skimmed the top, then flew off the end towards the beach.

The seal lunged at them but missed and crashed into the sign that said BEWARE LEOPARD SEALS.

Dude landed on the beach. With one flipper, he caught Amelia. With the other, he caught his surfboard. Every penguin on the beach was clapping and cheering. "Dude! Dude! Dude!" they cried.

Scott stood alone near the top of the cliff. He had watched the whole rescue. Of course, he was delighted that Amelia had been saved. He only wished it hadn't been by someone as cool and good-looking as Dude.

Dude took off his sunglasses. Amelia gazed up into his blue eyes. "My hero," she murmured and then she kissed him.

Chapter Six

At the end of the day, Scott trudged home with Humboldt. He was still upset about Amelia kissing Dude. Now she was Dude's "chick". He'd never thought about it before, but he realized that, deep down, he'd always wanted her to be his girlfriend.

"Are you listening to me? Scott?"

"Huh?" Scott muttered.

"I've been talking to you for the last five minutes," moaned Humboldt.

"Sorry. What about?"

"About our discovery, of course! About what's causing the heatwave. All Penguinville's got to hear about it. As soon as everyone knows that we're all in danger, then every penguin can work together to save the town."

They reached Scott's igloo. His dad, Principal Flipper, was flattening the snow lawn and shaping the ice hedges. "Hello, boys," he said.

"Principal Flipper," Humboldt squawked, "can you call a meeting in the school hall, please?"

"Whatever for?"

"Scott and I have an announcement to make. We've discovered what's causing the hot weather and we've got to do something about it straight away, or else there'll be big trouble."

"Big trouble?" sighed Principal Flipper. "And this big trouble is something you two have discovered all on your own?"

"Yes, sir," Humboldt replied.

"You run along home, Humboldt. Your parents will be wondering where you've got to. I'll talk to Scott about the meeting."

"Thanks, sir. Bye, sir." Humboldt waved and skipped up the street to his family's igloo.

"Now, Scott," said Principal Flipper, "what did I tell you about letting your imagination run away with you? Remember what happened to your grandfather? He wanted to be the first penguin to reach the South Pole and look what became of him! He made this family a laughing stock. It took me years and years of hard work as a schoolteacher, before everyone in Penguinville stopped making jokes about the Flippers."

"But, Dad, it isn't our imagination. What's happening to Penguinville is real. Will you call a meeting? Will you?"

Principal Flipper sighed. "I should ask Boss Beak first."

"He's the last penguin you should ask!"

"And what if you turn out to be wrong, son? Boss Beak'll have my gizzard for a garter."

"Dad, Boss Beak owns most of Penguinville. Does that mean he owns you, too?"

"No, son, of course he doesn't."

"Well, then." Scott gazed up at his dad with a pleading look.

Principal Flipper sighed. "I just know I'm going to regret this."

Scott threw himself into his father's flippers and gave him a big hug.

Chapter Seven

At the factory, Boss Beak peered down from his balcony. Thanks to Doctor Frost's new pipeline, production of Fishy Delight had returned to normal. All the fish might have gone from Penguinville Bay, but new supplies were being sucked in from the surrounding seas.

In spite of the heat, the workers weren't allowed to slow down. Sweat poured from their bodies until their feathers were soaked.

Boss Beak's security chief, Rocky Ice Berg, patrolled the factory floor, clumping from machine to machine and slapping a truncheon in his flipper. The workers were terrified of him. Ice had tattoos all the way up his flippers and his face was covered in scars. He said he'd got them in a wrestling match with a leopard seal. The seal had lost.

One of the workers was panting with

exhaustion. He stopped working, took out a bottle of water from his overall and gulped it down. Then he realized that Ice had seen him. "Mister Berg, please don't—"

Ice hoisted the worker into the air and carried him across the factory. His legs were kicking and he was squawking in terror. Ice dangled him over the Homogenizer.

The worker pleaded, "Please, Mister Berg, don't—!"

"SLACKERS MUST BE PUNISHED!" boomed Boss Beak from above.

Ice dropped the worker into the Homogenizer. The other penguins watched in horror. When they returned to work, they worked twice as hard.

Boss Beak nodded in approval. He ambled off the balcony and back into his office. A moment later, Biff strode in without knocking.

"If it isn't my idiot son," muttered Boss Beak. "What do *you* want?"

"Dad, trust me, you'll be proud of me this time."

"That'll be the day," said Boss Beak.

"Feast your eyes on this." Biff showed his father the page of scientific data that he'd stolen from Humboldt.

Boss Beak sucked on a cigar and blew out a cloud of smoke. "Big deal," he said. "My factory's been causing pollution for years."

"Oh," said Biff, taken by surprise. "You knew then?"

"Of course I did. And I don't care one bit. My job's to make money, not to worry about trivial things such as the environment. What's the environment ever done for me?"

"But, Dad, it looks like they're onto you."

Boss Beak shrugged. "When you're the most powerful penguin in town, no one can stop you doing anything, least of all a couple of nerdy kids."

"But I know what they're like, Dad. They take things seriously. I know they'll try and do something. But I'll stop them. You'll be proud of me at last, Dad. Leave it to me."

"Leave it to you?" Boss Beak laughed. "To you? You're the Penguinville playboy. Why, only last week, the newspapers were full of stories of you partying with film stars and dancing with supermodels. Parties are all you're good for." Boss Beak snatched the piece of paper out of Biff's flipper. "You mean about as much to me as a pile of guano. No, that's unfair – I can make money out of guano."

His dad had treated him this way for as long as Biff could remember. Whatever Biff achieved in his lessons, Boss Beak told him it wasn't good enough. He'd got much higher marks when he was his age. Whatever Biff wanted to do in life,

Boss Beak told him it was a waste of time. And if ever Biff *did* do a thing even remotely well, Boss Beak would tell him that thing couldn't be at all important.

Once upon a time, Boss Beak had been just an ordinary penguin, but he had worked very very hard to make the Beak Corporation the most successful business in Penguinville. "A lesser penguin would have been content to stop there," he'd once told Biff, "but not your father." He'd worked day and night, he'd lied and cheated and bullied, and now the Beak Corporation was the only business in Penguinville. "I own this town," he'd proclaimed and, quietly to himself, added, "and every penguin in it."

Biff had been born rich, yet he'd never made even a penny on his own. He sailed around in a yacht all day, but it was his dad's, not his. By comparison with his father, Biff was a complete failure. And Boss Beak never let a day pass without reminding him of it.

"You wait, Dad," Biff replied. "I'll show you what I'm made of. One day you'll be proud. You'll see."

Boss Beak had started signing some important documents. Biff waited, but his dad didn't look up. Tears welled in Biff's eyes. He shuffled out of the office and shut the door behind him.

Chapter Eight

The next day was hot too. The ice walls of the Penguinville school hall were dripping. Water trickled down to the floor and under the feet of the penguins who were scuttling in to hear about Scott and Humboldt's discovery. Cooling fans were turned up as high as they could go, and some were working so hard they had smoke coming out of their motors.

Amelia squeezed to the front of the hall. She watched Principal Flipper lead Scott and Humboldt onto the stage. Everyone had been chattering, but now they fell quiet.

Principal Flipper began, "Thank you all for coming this morning. My son Scott and his friend Humboldt have something extremely important to tell you all. Boys?"

Scott announced, "We've been studying the hot weather and we've found out what's causing it."

Humboldt consulted his pages of scientific data, and then he squawked, "There are two factors. Factor one: abundant chlorofluorocarbon emission is generating excessive chlorine radical formation in the stratosphere. Decomposition of the triatomic allotrope of oxygen is responsible for increased levels of solar ultraviolet radiation. Factor two: increased levels of carbon dioxide, methane and water vapour are causing an enhanced greenhouse effect. Heat from the sun is transmitted down to the ground in the form of high-frequency radiation. This radiation warms the ground, then the heat is emitted in the form of low-frequency infrared radiation. The carbon dioxide traps the infrared radiation..."

The penguins muttered to each other. No one could understand a word Humboldt was saying. Principal Flipper gave Scott a worried look. Scott knew he had to take over. He eased Humboldt aside, saying, "It's okay. I'll take it from here. You get the demonstration ready."

Scott turned to the audience. "It's very hot now," he explained, "because more sunlight than usual is shining on Penguinville. There's a gas in the sky high above us, gas called 'ozone'. Ozone protects us from the sun. We can't see it because it's invisible, like the air we breathe, but it's there above us like a screen. But the ozone is being destroyed by pollution, so more sunlight is being let through. There are other gases in the sky above us too. They're called 'carbon dioxide' and 'methane' and they're invisible too. They work like the windows of a greenhouse. They let sunlight through, and then trap the heat inside. That's why it's so hot in Penguinville at the moment. It's like we're living in a giant greenhouse."

Amelia was listening to every word. It was the first time she'd heard a young penguin talk to grown-ups about such important things. Scott was braver and cleverer than she'd thought.

The demonstration was ready. Humboldt had made a model of Penguinville out of ice cubes. Over the model of the town shone a lamp. Scott showed the model to the audience. "Imagine this lamp is the sun. It's shining down on Penguinville. Everything is normal. Everything is like it was a few months ago."

Humboldt picked up a test tube. It was the test tube that Scott had filled with factory fumes. The audience could see that there was a black gas inside.

Scott told them, "Now I'm going to show you what's happening today. I'm going to let this gas out of the test tube." He pulled out the stopper and the black gas flowed out between the lamp and the model of Penguinville. Gradually, the

49

ice cubes in the model Penguinville started to melt. Soon all the buildings were dripping and sinking into pools of water.

"But Penguinville isn't going to melt, is it?" shouted Amelia's father. "I mean – it *can't*."

"Yes it can," Scott replied. "It's going to get hotter and hotter. Eventually the heat will melt all the ice we live on. Penguinville will crumble into the sea."

The penguins were shocked. They were frightened. They started talking among themselves and soon the hall was filled with deafening squawks.

"Please, everyone, be calm!" begged Principal Flipper. "Citizens of Penguinville, *calm* yourselves!"

"But what's causing the heat?" shouted Amelia. "Is it the black gas?"

"Yes," Scott replied. The audience went quiet so everyone could listen. "The black gas in the test tube is pollution. Pollution is destroying the ozone layer and making our town like a greenhouse. We got this pollution from a place right here in Penguinville. We got this pollution from … the Beak Corporation factory."

Every penguin in the hall gasped.

Just then the doors at the back of the hall burst open. A sea of heads swung round to see Boss Beak filling the doorway. His cruel eyes tracked round the hall. A fearful silence gripped them all. Boss Beak lifted his gaze to the stage. He stared at Humboldt, who shuffled meekly behind his model of Penguinville. He stared at Principal Flipper, who started to speak but couldn't think of anything to say, so his beak just fell open. Then Boss Beak's stare came to rest on Scott. Scott trembled.

Chapter Nine

Boss Beak's eyes flicked back to Principal Flipper. "FLIPPER!" he roared. "HOW DARE YOU CALL A MEETING WITHOUT MY PER-MISSION?"

"Boss Beak, I er, I er..."

Boss Beak strode through the crowd. Penguins shuffled aside to let him through. He climbed onto the stage and turned to the audience. "Let me remind you, citizens of Penguin-ville," he boomed, "that my factory employs nearly all of you, and it makes every tin of Fishy Delight you eat, and there had better be a very *very* VERY good reason for you all being here."

Many of the penguins were trembling. Beaks were twitching from the front row all the way to the back of the hall.

Scott called out across the stage, "What's

more important – your factory or the fact that Penguinville is going to melt into the sea?"

The audience gasped. No penguin, absolutely no penguin, let alone a child, ever answered back to Boss Beak. Everyone expected him to fly into a rage.

Instead, he chuckled. He produced a sheet of paper from his waistcoat and held it up for everyone to see. "Citizens, I have here a copy of their so-called 'discovery'. Let's not forget that this is the work of children. I have shown their scientific data to my own expert grown-up scientists. I've shown it to Doctor Frost himself. My scientists have said that the hot weather could have happened at any time and for no particular reason. Things will soon return to normal. Citizens, be calm. There's absolutely nothing to worry about."

Great sighs of relief spread through the audience. Boss Beak smiled. He knew they'd believe him, if only because he was telling them exactly what they wanted to hear. A drop of water fell from the melting ceiling and splashed on his face. He wiped it away before anyone noticed.

"But what we say is *true*," Scott squawked. "Penguinville *is* melting. Our igloos are melting. Our streets are turning to slush. Only yesterday, the ice cliff crumbled and Amelia was nearly killed."

"Oh my, what a tragedy," sneered Boss Beak. "Citizens, the boy is right! I should put an end to this pollution. I should halt production of Fishy Delight today." He let his words register with the audience. Some of them were already nodding. Scott couldn't believe it. He shot Humboldt a huge grin of relief.

"But wait," Boss Beak continued, "if I stop making Fishy Delight, what would we eat? Who here would like a plate of seaweed for his dinner? Or moss perhaps? I wouldn't."

He stared at all the penguin faces in the audience. To the Beach Café manager he said, "Would you?" The Beach Café manager shook his head.

To Amelia's father he said, "Would you?" Amelia's father shook his head.

To Humboldt's mother he said, "Would you?" Humboldt's mother shook her head.

Boss Beak turned back to Scott in triumph. "You see!" he cried. "What would life be like without a delicious supper of Fishy Delight of an evening? Well? What would it be like?"

"There won't be *any* life here soon," Scott replied, "and stopping the pollution won't make a difference." His voice was grim and he fought to keep control of his emotions. "The damage has already been done. The climate has changed. It won't return to normal for decades, maybe centuries, maybe even not at all. By then it'll be too late. Penguinville will have melted – just like the icebergs that float out to sea and never come back."

Silence fell on the hall. Scott had painted a bleak and terrifying picture. It was nothing short of the end of the world. It was penguin apocalypse.

Scott continued, "The only hope for us penguins is to move somewhere colder. A place so cold it will never melt."

"And where might that be?" Boss Beak snorted.

"The South Pole of course," Scott answered.

Boss Beak started to laugh. "The South Pole! No penguin has attempted the journey in more than thirty years – not since Shackleton Flipper's ill-considered and ill-fated expedition."

The penguins muttered their agreement.

From a back corner of the hall, Henson staggered towards the stage. He slurred, "Shackleton Flipper *did* reach the South Pole. I saw him set out from Base Camp Albatross into that blizzard. The albatross! The albatross!"

The audience laughed and jeered.

Boss Beak's voice rode the jeers. "And what is there for us penguins at the South Pole?" he demanded. "A wasteland, that's what! Penguins have always lived on the *coast*. We need the sea for our fish. We don't belong inland. We certainly don't belong in a bleak freezing wasteland!"

"No, listen to me!" Scott cried. "The climate of Penguinville has got hotter. I think that must mean the South Pole has got warmer too, so it'll be just right for us."

Boss Beak boomed with laughter. "You 'think' it 'must mean' the South Pole will be 'just right'? You're admitting that you don't know for certain?"

Scott trembled. "Well I ... how can anyone know for certain ... unless they go there ... and see for themselves?"

"Then you don't *know*!"

Scott gulped. "But I've got a ... feeling."

"Listen to him, townspenguins!" cried Boss Beak. "He wants us to abandon our homes and cross a harsh wilderness of unknown terrors! The one lunatic who tried never came back. He wants us to waddle to our certain deaths, all because he has a 'feeling'!"

The penguins' laughter shook the school hall. Scott glanced sadly at Humboldt and at his father.

Boss Beak put a flipper to his breast. "Penguins," he said solemnly, "we should pity him. This boy, Scott, is suffering from the same madness that afflicted his grandfather all those years ago. Why would anyone ever want to leave Penguinville? We have all we could ever want right here. Besides, any day now, the weather will go back to normal. So why worry? Now, every penguin back to work!"

Then he strode out of the hall and the penguins trooped after him.

Principal Flipper looked down at Scott. "You know, son," he said, "ever since you were an egg, I've dreaded the day you'd take after your grandfather." He followed the other penguins out of the hall.

Soon only Henson and Amelia were left looking up at the stage. Scott couldn't believe what had happened. He was sadder than he'd ever been in his life – and angrier too.

Humboldt shuffled to his side and patted him on the back. "You did the best you could," he said.

Amelia mounted the stage. Scott looked so sad and alone that she wanted to help him, though she didn't know how.

Just then Dude strolled in. "Hey guys, did I miss something?" he asked.

"Oh Dude," moaned Amelia, "you *promised* you'd be here."

"Gee sorry, babe. I was waxin' my board." Dude pecked Amelia on the beak.

She blushed. "I forgive you, darling."

"I know our data is correct," wailed Humboldt. "Boss Beak's scientists are the ones who are wrong, not us."

"This is just like grown-ups," Amelia squawked. "They're so selfish. They never care about the future. They won't do anything to stop Penguinville being destroyed because it'll only be us kids who'll really suffer."

"My chick's right," Dude drawled. "You can try tellin' the grown-ups stuff but, man, they never do listen."

"We can't let them beat us," Scott declared. "This is too important. By the time they find out they were wrong, Penguinville will have melted."

"What are you saying, Scott?" Amelia asked.

Scott replied, "I'm saying that the only way of saving penguinkind is to prove to the grown-ups that the South Pole can be our new home. And the only way of doing that" – Scott gulped – "is to go there."

Dude pulled a face. "Man, you know, that sounds like, you know, *hard* work."

Humboldt and Amelia gazed at Scott.

"Can we manage it?" Amelia asked. "Really Scott? Can we succeed?"

Scott searched for an answer. In truth, he didn't know if they could – they were just a bunch of kids.

Then Henson cried, "Are you not Scott Flipper, grandson of the great Shackleton Flipper? Other penguins may inherit wealth or property, but you've been given something far more valuable."

Henson stumbled onto the stage. He took out the faded old photograph of Shackleton and gave it to Scott.

Scott gazed down at the thirty-year-old picture of the bearded penguin wearing tweeds and furs.

Henson said, "You have inherited the heart and mind of an *explorer*. Scott, are you ready to live up to your birthright?"

Everyone looked at him.

Scott cradled the photo of Shackleton Flipper. He'd seen it many times before, but this time it seemed as if the old explorer's eyes were looking out at him from the past. He could feel his grandfather's spirit reaching out across the years, urging him to take the first big step. Scott took a deep breath. Then he said for all to hear, "I'm ready."

Chapter Ten

Scott, Amelia, Dude and Humboldt thought they were alone in the school hall with Henson. But hiding under the stage, listening to every word, were Biff and Brittany.

They heard the four plan their expedition to the South Pole. Henson was too old and drunk to come with them, but he could draw them a map. Dude would cut up firewood and borrow tents from the lifeguard station. Humboldt would collect anoraks, furs, boots and snow goggles. Amelia would put lots of food in a rucksack for the journey. Scott would study his grandfather's journals to find out everything he could about polar exploration.

Biff and Brittany heard Scott say, "It's decided. We'll meet here at dawn tomorrow. By the time our parents find out we're gone, we'll be on our way to the South Pole." There was the sound of Scott, Amelia, Humboldt and Dude slapping their flippers in high fives, and then of their footsteps as they crept out of the hall.

When they were sure it was safe, Biff and Brittany crawled out from under the stage.

"OK," said Biff. "We'll set off tomorrow morning too, an hour before dawn. That way we can ambush them as they leave town."

Brittany shook her head in disbelief. "Tomorrow? I've got an appointment with my featherstylist. I'm busy all week. In fact, I'm busy for the rest of my life. Sorry Biff. If you want to stop them saving Penguinville, you're on your own."

"Who cares about Penguinville?" Biff squawked. "I don't care about anything but myself. If they succeed in proving we'd all be better off at the South Pole, that'll be the end of the Beak Corporation. My father will lose his fortune. That means there'll be no money *for me*. And that means there'll be no expensive dresses and jewellery *for you*."

Brittany didn't have to think for very long. "Tomorrow morning, an hour before dawn? No problem."

That night, while Scott, Amelia, Humboldt and Dude got ready for their expedition, Biff and Brittany got ready for theirs.

Chapter Eleven

An alarm clock sounded in Beak Mansion. It went off for no more than a couple of seconds before Biff silenced it with a flick of his flipper. He sat up in his nest and listened out for signs that the alarm had woken the rest of the household. When he was sure everyone was still asleep, he slipped out of his nest. He put on a coat, a hat, gloves and a scarf. Hidden at the bottom of his wardrobe was a large rucksack filled with supplies and equipment, which he hoisted onto his back.

Then he paused. He took out a pen and paper and wrote a note. He slipped it into an envelope, which he addressed *To Dad*, and laid it on his pillow.

Biff Beak stepped out into the grounds of Beak Mansion. The sky was still pitch-black. His breath made white puffs of condensation in the cold air. The crisp snow crunched under his feet as he set off to rendezvous with Brittany.

Brittany was fast asleep in her nest. Her alarm had gone off more than a dozen times without waking her. There was a loud rap on the ice pane of her nestroom window. Brittany stirred. The rapping got louder and she jolted awake.

"Who's there?" she whispered.

"Get up," came an impatient voice.

Brittany swept open the curtains. Biff was crouching on the window ledge outside, looking annoyed.

"I overslept," Brittany explained.

"Just hurry up. We're going to be late."

Brittany blinked at her reflection in the mirror. "Just look at the bags under my eyes," she moaned. "I'm not taking a single step towards the South Pole until I've put on my make-up."

Biff glanced at his watch, and sighed miserably.

By the time Biff and Brittany reached the outskirts of Penguinville, the sun had risen. They'd taken off their coats and hats and gloves. Their breath no longer condensed into white clouds. Instead they panted in the warm air. They ached under the weight of their rucksacks.

"Are we in time for the ambush?" Brittany wondered.

"In time?"

"Is it an hour before dawn yet?"

Biff pointed at the sun. "Darling, do you see that big bright thing in the sky?"

"The sun?"

"That's right. And it's kind of a major clue that it's not *before* dawn."

Brittany huffed. "Don't blame me. This was your plan, not mine."

Biff noticed marks in the snow nearby. There were four sets of penguin footprints, all heading out of town, all heading south. "We've missed them," he growled and threw down his rucksack in annoyance.

"Good," said Brittany. "This silliness is over with then. We can go home."

Behind them the town of Penguinville lay melting in the morning sun. Ahead was a vast wilderness that no penguin had lived to describe. All Biff's cowardly instincts told him to turn back towards home, but that was precisely what his father would expect of him. He'd expect him to fail. Now was the time to prove once and for all that he was a better penguin than that.

"No," he said. He picked up his rucksack and swung it over his shoulders. "Let's get after them."

Chapter Twelve

Back in Penguinville, the senior lifeguard went looking for Dude. He saw someone perched at the top of the ladder, hidden under a towel. Thinking Dude was nesting on the job, he climbed up and pulled away the towel. Dude wasn't there. Instead there was just the flagpole with a bucket stuck on it to look like his head.

When Humboldt's mother went into his nestroom to wake him up, she could hear snoring coming from under his nestclothes. "Time for mummy's little genius to wake up," she called. Humboldt didn't move. His mother pulled away the covers. Humboldt wasn't in his nest. Instead pillows heaped up the blankets and a tape recorder was playing the snoring sounds.

Amelia's mother and father were eating breakfast. "Amelia!" her mother called up the stairs. "Your breakfast's ready! Amelia?" There was no reply. Amelia's mother looked upstairs, then she ran out into the street.

Principal Flipper was already there. "Have you seen Amelia?" Amelia's mother asked.

"No I haven't." Principal Flipper looked up the street and down. "Have you seen Scott?"

"No I haven't."

It was Humboldt's mother's turn to rush out into the street. "Has anyone seen Humboldt?" she asked.

"No," said Principal Flipper and Amelia's mother.

The senior lifeguard chugged by in his beach buggy. "Has anyone seen Dude?" he asked.

"No," said Principal Flipper and Amelia's mother and Humboldt's mother.

They all looked at each other. "Where could they have got to?" asked Amelia's mother.

"Let's not start worrying just yet," said Principal Flipper. "Wherever they are, I'm sure it's nowhere dangerous."

At exactly that moment, far down the coast from Penguinville Bay, huge waves were crashing against a cliff. The wind howled. Snow fell from the sky in thick clumps. And high, high up on a narrow ridge of ice, four young penguins were waddling towards the South Pole.

Chapter Thirteen

The penguins had left home at dawn. As soon as they were out of Penguinville, Humboldt looked down at his compass. The needle swung and, when it came to a stop, he pointed into the icy wastes. "That way," he said. "South."

Looking at the compass every hour or so and following Henson's map, they trudged all day through wind and snow. The further south they went, the colder it became. They loved being back in cold weather. As Dude said 'Cold is so cool.'

But now they were very tired. Night was falling. Stars were appearing in the darkening sky. They pitched their four tents in the enormous silent wilderness. Scott took his camera out of his rucksack. Henson had told him that it was very important to keep a record of the expedition for penguins to look at in years to come. So Amelia, Dude and Humboldt stood together in front of their tents and Scott set up the picture. He clicked the timer and joined his friends. A few seconds later the camera flashed.

Then the silence was broken. There was someone outside the camp. In the darkness the four penguins couldn't see anything, but they could hear heavy breathing.

Amelia trembled. "What's that?"

The breathing got louder.

"Snow monsters?" suggested Humboldt.

Scott picked up a walking pole. "Whatever they are," he said, "they're coming this way. Protect yourselves."

The others picked up poles too. The breathing sounds were very loud. Scott and Dude gripped their skis, ready for action.

Out of the darkness came a voice. "Help us!" Then Biff and Brittany crawled into the camp and collapsed in the snow.

Amelia sighed. "There goes the neighbourhood."

"Fluky or what!" Dude exclaimed. "Are you guys on an expedition to the South Pole too?"

Biff and Brittany struggled out of their heavy rucksacks. They lay in the snow, too weary even to sit up. Scott stood over them. "What are you two doing here?" he demanded.

"We wanted to join your expedition," Biff

gasped. "But it's been harder work than we expected. We're both dead beat. And hungry. Can we have some food?"

"In return for what?"

"Like I said, we want to join your expedition. We've come to lend our services."

"Whatever they are, they're not needed," said Scott.

Biff gasped for breath. "Scotty old chum, listen to us, please. I'm sorry for the way I've treated you all in the past. I'm sorry my dad wouldn't listen to you. But it's time to forget all that." He held up his flipper.

Scott refused Biff's flippershake.

Dude started unpacking Biff's rucksack. He found a really great snow hat and put it on. He pulled out more clothing and equipment. "Wow guys," he cried. "No bogus brands here. This stuff's really going to help us get to the Pole – and *in style*!"

Humboldt whispered to Scott, "I hate Biff and Brittany as much as anyone, but we do need all the help we can get."

By now, Dude was trying on ski jackets and gloves.

"Scott," Biff continued, "you really convinced us at the meeting in the school hall. We penguins have to work together to find a cold new home. We can't afford to be enemies, if we're going to save penguinkind."

"You don't believe him, do you?" Amelia asked Scott.

"It's the truth," Biff said.

"Okay," Scott sighed and shook Biff's flipper.

"You won't regret this," Biff told him.

At the bottom of Biff's rucksack, Dude found six sticks of dynamite. "Whoa guys! Dynamite! This expedition's going to be a *blast*."

Scott shook his head. "I think I'm already beginning to regret this."

Chapter Fourteen

The next morning, the penguins continued their journey. All the extra equipment Biff and Brittany had brought was piled onto a sledge. A rope went from the sledge round each penguin's waist and, as a team, they trudged through the snow dragging it behind them.

It was getting a lot colder. The tips of their beaks and the tips of their flippers turned blue. "This weather is gorgeous," Amelia trilled, and everyone squawked in agreement.

Scott and Humboldt looked at Henson's map. It was covered in smudges, and even the lines that were supposed to be straight had come out wiggly.

Humboldt took out his compass and waited for the needle to stop swinging. When it did, he pointed into snowy wilderness. "That way," he said. "South."

Soon they were crossing a sheet of ice near the edge of the sea. Biff saw that it was actually a bridge between two pieces of land. It looked weak and probably wouldn't be able to take their weight.

He stopped to let Dude go first. "After you, old chum," he said cheerily.

"Thanks, man," said Dude.

Scott saw Dude step onto the bridge. "Now remember, everyone," he called, "always, always test the ice before you—"

Dude clumped his foot down hard.

The bridge collapsed. Dude plunged towards the sea. His section of rope pulled Biff after him, and Biff's section of rope pulled Humboldt, and Humboldt's pulled Brittany, and Brittany's pulled Amelia, and Amelia's pulled Scott. All the penguins fell squawking into the sea. The bridge crashed after them, and then bobbed up like an iceberg. The penguins clambered aboard.

"You all OK?" Scott called.

Amelia spoke for everyone, "Seems like we've had a lucky escape."

"Thank heavens," said Biff, but he thumped the iceberg with his flipper. Under his breath he whispered, "Next time, you won't be so lucky."

"I'd hardly say we were lucky!" exclaimed Brittany. "Look – I've broken a nail!"

Amelia threw a handful of slush at her.

"Hey!" shouted Brittany. "I saw that!"

"Spoilt little princess," hissed Amelia.

"Shush!" Scott commanded. The iceberg was floating away from land. "We've got to do something to stop ourselves drifting out to sea. We're in a real mess – thanks to Dude."

"Chill out, dude," said Dude. "Wait, I'm 'Dude'. I mean, 'cool it, *man*'. And don't go shushing my chick. That's so, like, uptight."

"I'm 'uptight'," Scott squawked, "because you've got us stranded on an iceberg that's floating in exactly the opposite direction to where we're supposed to be going. I said nobody was to step onto the ice till they'd tested it."

Dude shrugged. "Man, you gotta admit those are pretty complicated instructions."

"Wait," Amelia interrupted. "I think the wind's changing."

Sure enough, a gust of wind was turning the iceberg back towards land. Before long the wind was blowing them along at a good speed, and they were travelling in a southerly direction.

The wind got stronger. Soon they were sailing ten times faster than they could ever have waddled.

"What was that you were saying, Scott?" Dude gloated. "Seems like the iceberg was actually an awesome manoeuvre by the dudester."

Amelia leaned towards Dude and gave him a kiss. "My hero," she murmured.

Scott scowled. "I'll try and work out what we do next. Humboldt, take lookout."

"Aye aye, skipper!" said Humboldt, inching to the front of the iceberg and scanning the sea ahead for danger.

Dude put his flipper round Amelia. As they sailed along, they looked at the scenery. There were tall cliffs of ice. Fish were leaping in and out of the water. The sea was blue and gleamed like a mirror. Amelia murmured, "Whisper sweet nothings in my ear."

"Er…" Dude leaned close to her ear, and said, "Sweet nothings."

"No, Dude," Amelia wailed, "what I mean is … do you think I'm pretty?"

"Sure you are, doll."

"Then why don't you ever say it?"

"Er … you're pretty," said Dude.

"Pretty as what?"

"Hmm." Dude tried to think. "Pretty as a … brand new superwaxed surfboard."

"Oh," Amelia said, disappointed.

Dude stared hard into the sea, desperately trying to think of something romantic to say. He thought so hard that he feared his head would explode.

Amelia could see that he was thinking very

hard about something. "Dude," she asked, "are you like an iceberg?"

"Pointy and made of ice?"

"No, silly! Is there more to you than meets the eye?"

"Huh?"

"You know," Amelia explained, "we only see the tip of an iceberg. Most of it is under the water. So you're the strong silent type."

"Oh!" said Dude. "Now I get you, doll. You must think I'm a total birdbrain." Blushing with embarrassment, he shuffled along the iceberg to be alone. Amelia frowned. She always seemed to say the wrong thing. Instead of getting more relaxed with her as they spent more time together, Dude actually seemed to be getting more tongue-tied.

Scott crossed the iceberg. "I'm sorry I blamed you for us falling into the sea, Dude," he said. "We're a team. We've got to stick up for each other, no matter what."

"Thanks dude," said Dude, and they shook flippers. Scott was about to turn away when Dude added, "You know man, Amelia must think I'm a total chowderhead. I can never think what to say to her. Hey, I've got it! You've known her longer than me. You know the kinda stuff she's in to. *You* could tell me clever stuff I can use on her."

Scott wanted nothing more than for Amelia to get fed up with Dude. Now Dude was asking for his help. "Dude," said Scott, "it's only fair – er, *fair on Amelia*, I mean – that she finds out you might not be the right penguin for her."

"What did you just say about being a team?" Dude squawked. "You said we should stick together, no matter what. I'm helping you reach the stupid South Pole. So in return, you should help me impress my chick."

"I suppose you're right," Scott sighed. "I'll think of something."

"Thanks a million, man," said Dude and slapped him on the back so hard that Scott nearly fell into the sea.

Chapter Fifteen

The penguins clung onto the iceberg as it carried them down the coast. Biff and Brittany were whispering to each other. "Look what you've done," Brittany muttered. "You haven't stopped them. You've *helped* them."

"You know who you sound like?" Biff growled. "My dad." He marched to the opposite side of the iceberg and sat with his legs dangling over the edge, staring out to sea.

Amelia joined Scott and Humboldt. "I know this is a stupid question," she began, "but what exactly *is* the South Pole?"

"It's the most southerly place there is," Scott explained. "It's the bottom of the world. If you go south from anywhere and keep going south till you can get no further, then that's the South Pole."

Amelia mused. "How do you tell which way

is south?" she asked.

"With this," said Humboldt. He showed her his compass. "The world is like a giant magnet. It makes the needle on the compass swing round till it points north. So then you know that the opposite direction must be south." Humboldt showed Amelia that the compass needle was pointing out to sea. He pointed back towards land. "That way."

"In fact," Scott interrupted, "that's exactly where we're heading." He'd noticed that the iceberg was being blown back onto the coast. "Everyone hold tight! We're going to run aground!"

A scraping noise rose from the bottom of the iceberg. It jolted and twisted, throwing the penguins to the ground. They clung on and, a few seconds later, the iceberg came to rest only a short hop from the shore.

"OK, everyone," Scott commanded, "time to get off."

The penguins lined up to jump. Dude ran across the iceberg and flung himself through the air. He hit the shore, slipped, spun beak over tail and skidded into a snowdrift. Amelia gulped, but made the leap. Scott, Humboldt and Biff followed.

While Brittany dithered. Humboldt got out Henson's map. He looked at the shape of the coast and the mountains in the distance, and then back at the map. "We're *miles* further along!" he exclaimed. "I calculate it would have taken us four days to get this far."

"*Four days*," Brittany repeated to Biff.

"Come on, princess," Amelia squawked, "everyone's waiting."

In a huff, Brittany took four paces backwards, then made her run-up. Her jump fell short. She hit the shore and flopped back into the water. She splashed in the icy sea, spitting out beakfuls of water, until Dude hoisted her out.

"I'm soaking wet!" she spluttered. "My feathers are a mess!"

Amelia couldn't help sniggering. "We all have bad-feather days."

"You more than most, dear," Brittany sneered.

Amelia flung a flipperful of slush at her.

"That's it!" Brittany wailed, "I've had enough of this sappy South Pole safari!"

"Then go home, princess!" Amelia squawked. "No one invited you in the first place."

While everyone watched the argument between Amelia and Brittany, Biff took a small object out of his rucksack pocket. It was a tiny magnet. He looked round to make sure no one was watching, then quickly opened Humboldt's rucksack and stuck it onto the back of the compass.

Scott ended the argument between Amelia and Brittany. "Enough, you two! We're a team now. We all stick together." He turned to Humboldt. "We have to carry on south. Which way now?"

Biff held his breath as Humboldt took the compass out of his rucksack. Humboldt didn't notice the tiny magnet stuck on the back of it. Biff smiled behind his flipper.

The compass needle swung round, first one way, then the other. Humboldt frowned. There seemed to be something wrong with it. Then, just as he was about to say something, the needle came to a stop. He peered into the distance. Snow and ice covered the land ahead. The wind blew in their faces. A mountain rose up from the plain. It was shaped like a craggy pyramid, coated with snow and its summit was so high that it disappeared in cloud. Humboldt pointed past the mountain. "That way," he said.

"Are you sure?" Scott wondered.

"That's what the compass says," Humboldt replied.

The penguins hoisted their rucksacks onto their shoulders and piled the rest of their equipment on the sledge. Scott commemorated the next stage of the expedition by taking a photograph of all six penguins with the mountain as a background.

"OK," said Scott, "we've got a lot of terrain to cover before night. I'll lead. Biff, take flank. Let's ship out, team."

He set off at the front of the line. The others followed. Right at the back was Biff. He knew they were going the wrong way and smiled to himself.

Chapter Sixteen

The expedition to the South Pole was plunging into colder and colder lands but, in Penguin-ville, the weather was getting hotter.

From dawn till dusk, the sun scorched the town. There was no breeze. The air was stifling. Penguinville Hospital was treating the worst cases of sunburn and heatstroke any of the doctors had ever seen. Many of the smaller igloos were melting so badly the families had to move out. The streets were turning into rivers. The Hard Frost Café had melted, as had McDonald's Iceberger Restaurant. The cinema, which had been showing *The Refrigerator* starring Arnold Penguinegger, had flooded. Only a few days after Scott and Humboldt had warned the penguins about what was going to happen, Penguinville School's classrooms had melted. The roof of the gym had fallen in and one side of the hall had collapsed.

Scott's parents, Humboldt's parents and Amelia's parents plodded waist-deep in water, up to the Beak Corporation factory. Sweat made their feathers soggy. They were panting in the heat. By the time they were shown into Boss Beak's office, the mothers were crying. The fathers tried to be brave, but they had tears in their eyes too.

Boss Beak's office was like the inside of a freezer. "Isn't it lovely and cold?" commented Principal Flipper.

"I've had air conditioning installed," Boss Beak replied. "It's a constant minus forty in here." Boss Beak lit a fresh cigar and blew out a cloud of smoke. It froze to crystals that twinkled and then tinkled to the floor. "So what do you want?" he demanded.

"Boss Beak," said Principal Flipper, "we thought if anyone had heard, you would have. Is there any news?"

On Boss Beak's desk lay the letter Biff had left on his pillow before setting off. It said:

Dear Sir (Dad),

I have discovered that Scott Flipper and his friends are going to the South Pole.

I will ~~sabu~~ ~~sabutage~~ ~~sabot~~
ruin their ~~expadit~~
~~expodition~~ trip. I will prove
to you what I'm made of.

You'll be proud of me, Dad.
  Yours faithfully,
    your loyal son,
      Biff

Boss Beak hid the letter. "I'm afraid there's been no news," he announced gravely. "I haven't the faintest idea what's happened to your children."

All the parents sobbed.

"As you know," Boss Beak squawked, "I'm a very busy penguin. So go away."

"Of course, sir," said Amelia's father. "Thank you for finding the time to see us."

"And what about my son's warning?" Principal Flipper asked. "Meaning no disrespect, sir, but are your scientists sure this heatwave won't last?"

"They're absolutely certain," Boss Beak replied. "There's nothing at all to worry about." He waved them away and started signing a pile of important documents.

When the parents had gone, he pushed a button on his desk and, a few minutes later, Doctor Frost rolled into the office in his motorized wheelchair. "You called, Boss Beak?"

"The expedition to the South Pole cannot be allowed to succeed. If those kids come back and tell everyone we'd be better off living there, then I'm finished. My idiot son thinks he can stop them, but he's sure to find some way of messing it up. I shall have to stop them myself."

"But Boss Beak, they have been gone for days. No ordinary penguin could catch up with them now."

"You're right, Doctor Frost," said Boss Beak. He sucked his cigar, and blew out smoke. "No *ordinary* penguin could." He pressed the buzzer on his desk. "SECURITY!" he roared.

Ice Berg, the fearsome security chief, stomped through the door.

"Berg," commanded Boss Beak, "you will travel directly south till you find a group of six penguin children. You will do whatever is required to stop them reaching the South Pole. I repeat, whatever is required."

Ice grinned at the prospect of causing mayhem. He had a deep laugh that came out in short bursts. "Hur-hur-hur-hur," he went, then paused for a few seconds, then went, "Hur-hur-

hur-hur," again. He carried on like that for over a minute.

Doctor Frost whispered, "But Boss Beak, he could kill them – your son included."

"No one made them go to the South Pole," sighed Boss Beak. "Every penguin knows it's certain death. They only have themselves to blame."

Then both of them, Boss Beak and Doctor Frost, began to cackle madly.

"Hur-hur-hur-hur," went Ice.

Chapter Seventeen

Far away from Penguinville, snow and ice covered the land. The penguins leaned into the wind, dragging their equipment behind them. They trudged all day and then made camp. The next day they carried on. Soon the tall craggy pyramid-shaped mountain was behind them. They marched down into a huge canyon of ice. By the evening, they had travelled so far, they couldn't see the mountain any more.

They stopped and put up their tents. Humboldt looked at Henson's map. Though he couldn't be sure, he thought they were already halfway to the South Pole. Everyone cheered.

Biff started to laugh.

"What's so funny?" Humboldt asked.

"Nothing," Biff replied. "I'm just happy everything's going so smoothly." Then he went into his tent, where no one could see him or hear him, and carried on laughing.

Amelia squatted in the snow to watch the sun set. She thought the penguins were lucky to live in such a beautiful land. It was the most beautiful place on Earth. The possibility that one day it might all be destroyed made her so sad she wanted to weep.

Scott crouched down beside her. He watched the sun set too. He found that he was thinking the same thing as her. He couldn't be sure, of course. He just seemed to *know* that he was. If the expedition failed, penguin life might come to an end and the beauty around them might be gone for ever. Tears welled up in his eyes.

"Scott?" said Amelia. "What's wrong?"

"My grandpa tried what we're trying," he answered, "and he never came back. I was just thinking that we can't afford to fail. And I suppose I was thinking how scared I am."

"I'm scared too," said Amelia. She didn't know why, but she felt like reaching out to Scott. She put her flipper round him, giving him a little hug.

Dude coughed loudly behind them. Amelia quickly pulled her flipper away and Scott jumped to his feet.

"Need to talk to you, man," said Dude, and he beckoned Scott to the other side of the camp.

Scott spluttered, "Really Dude, there was

nothing going on between Amelia and me—"

"Quiet, man, and listen," said Dude. "Beautiful sunset. Amelia sat there on her own. This has gotta be where the dudester makes his move. So what do I say?"

"Give me a couple of minutes," said Scott.

He pulled out his notebook and gazed at Amelia, who was still watching the sunset. Scott thought that she looked more beautiful than ever. He loved her. If there was something he could do to make her dump Dude, then he was going to do it. He scribbled quickly in his notebook and then passed it over.

"What's this, man?" Dude asked.

"A poem."

"A poem!" Dude gasped. "Chicks so dig poems! Scott, man, you're my main penguin."

Then he scampered towards Amelia and plonked himself down beside her. "Hi babe," he said. "The last few days, I been thinkin' I don't say enough of the lovey-dovey stuff to you, so I've written you a poem."

"A poem? Dude, that's so romantic."

Scott watched from his tent. He knew he'd done a bad thing, but he believed that it was for the best.

"This comes straight from my heart," said Dude. He cleared his throat and began to read.

"Amelia, you are so pretty, kind and sweet.
Yet I'm just this useless slab of meat.
Beauty like yours should be praised and adored,
But all I'm good for is waxing my board.

Why put up with a boy who'll lounge and loaf,
When you can do better than this muscle-bound oaf?

Amelia, I've not got the slightest brain in my head,
So you should go out with Scott instead."

Scott couldn't wait to see Amelia's reaction. She was bound to dump Dude now and go out with him instead. To his amazement, Amelia smiled up at Dude.

"So that's why you've found it so hard to tell me how you feel," she murmured. "You don't think you're good enough for me. Dude, you're so humble. You make me feel such a special penguin."

Amelia kissed Dude. Scott couldn't believe it.

The sun set at last. Night fell on the camp. Scott zipped shut his tent and cried himself to sleep.

Chapter Eighteen

In the morning, Scott got up before any of the others. He pressed snow on his eyes, which were still red and swollen. By sunrise they looked normal again and no one could tell he'd been crying. Scott told himself that Amelia would never love him. Dude was her boyfriend and he had to learn to live with it. His job was to get the penguins to the South Pole and back. If they failed, all of penguinkind would suffer. That was far more important than the happiness of one little boy penguin like him.

"Everybody up!" Scott squawked into the tents. He kicked snow over the remains of last night's supper.

The other penguins waddled out into the morning light. They rolled up their tents and loaded their rucksacks.

Brittany looked at her reflection in a compact

mirror and put her make-up on.

Amelia sighed, "Brittany, *princess*, we're in wilderness. No one's going to be painting your portrait today."

"A girl should always make the best of her appearance," said Brittany. "Not that you'd know, being such a tomboy."

Amelia growled.

Humboldt checked the compass against the map and pointed ahead. "That way," he said. "South."

"South, yes," repeated Biff and hid his smirk with a flipper.

In a line, tied together with rope, the penguins trudged out into the icy wastes. Before long clouds smothered the sun. The wind started to howl. Snow began falling and the penguins put on their goggles.

"A blizzard," said Amelia. "Lovely."

"This is paradise," added Scott. "If the South Pole is even half this cold, it'll be the perfect place to live."

"I haven't felt so cold in ages," agreed Humboldt, buttoning up his anorak for the first time in a very long while.

Dude peered ahead. Everything was getting whiter and whiter. He could hear the wind and the crunching of their boots in the snow, but he couldn't see a thing. "Man, it's all so white."

Amelia laughed. "Silly – the snow's sticking to your goggles." She wiped them clean with her flipper. "See?"

"Oh yeah, that's better," said Dude. He gazed ahead. "Wow, that mountain looks exactly like the one we passed a few days ago."

Amelia peered up at the craggy outline of the pyramid-shaped mountain. "It *is* the one," she gasped.

The line of penguins slowed to a standstill. They all stared at the mountain. "We've been going in a circle," Scott snapped.

Humboldt stuttered, "But, but – I, I – we *can't* have—"

Biff snatched Humboldt's compass. He shook it. Without anyone noticing, he slipped off the tiny magnet and slid it back in his pocket. The compass needle swung round and came to a stop. Ahead was north, not south. "You fool," he squawked at Humboldt, "you've been reading it wrongly all this time!"

"But – but – the compass can't have been working properly," Humboldt protested.

"Sure – it was the compass," Brittany sighed sarcastically.

"I don't know how I could've got it wrong—" Humboldt said. Then he fell silent and started to cry.

Scott put a flipper round his friend's

shoulders. "Humboldt, there's no use blaming yourself," he said. "Plot a new course for the South Pole."

"Maybe someone else should?" Humboldt sobbed.

"No. I trust you to get it right. Go on. Please."

"OK, Scott." Humboldt wiped his beak and began to study the map.

Brittany moaned, "My feet are aching and my feathers have never been so out of condition. I've got split ends. I want to go home."

"I couldn't agree more," said Biff. "We're tired. We've already eaten most of our food. The terrain's getting harder. I say, 'Back to Penguinville!'"

Amelia wailed, "If we don't reach the South Pole, there *won't* be a Penguinville!"

"This is madness!" Biff squawked. "Look around you! Look around you! Look around you!" He flung his flippers in all directions. "It might be wonderfully freezingly cold, but this is a huge great empty nothing. How could we ever live here? We'd all be better off in Penguinville, whether it's melting or not. At least there's the seaside. At least there's food. So I say, 'Let's turn back right away.'"

"Your family might run things in Penguinville," Scott replied, "but out here you're not the one who gives the orders."

"And you are, I suppose?" said Biff.

"Yes I am."

"And you're responsible for everything that goes on."

"Yes I am."

"You chose Humboldt to be our navigator, so it's your fault that we've been going the wrong way. So I say, 'Let's choose a new leader.'"

"I choose Biff," piped Brittany.

"We should stick by Scott," said Humboldt, glancing up from the map.

Everyone turned to Dude and Amelia.

"This is silly," said Biff. "Now Amelia's going to choose Dude and we'll be split into three pairs."

Dude puffed out his breast. "No one's ever said I could give orders before. *Cool.*"

"We're in the middle of nowhere," said Brittany, "and we can't even agree on a leader. Some expedition! Who cares who leads? Let's just go home before we starve."

"Hey," squawked Amelia, sticking her flippers on her hips. "How come everyone's assuming I'll choose Dude, just because he's my boyfriend? We might've gone the wrong way, but we're all safe and we're all a team, thanks to Scott. I trust him to lead us to the South Pole. I choose Scott to be leader. Dude, who do you think is the best penguin for the job?"

Dude shrugged. "Scott, I guess."

"Sorry Biff," Amelia concluded. "Humboldt, Dude and I all vote for Scott. If you and Brittany want to go home no one's stopping you, but the rest of us are going on."

Scott looked at Amelia. No one had ever stuck up for him like that. Well, Humboldt had, but Humboldt was a little geek with glasses. Amelia was the most beautiful penguin in the world and she wanted him to lead the expedition. *She wanted him* (to lead the expedition).

"You OK, man?" Dude asked Scott. "You got some kinda real dopey grin on your face."

Scott wiped the schoolboy-in-love smirk from his face and tried to look serious and determined and leader-like. "OK everyone, let's move on."

"Where to?" Biff demanded.

The penguins were weary. Their food was running out. The terrain was getting more desolate. Despite himself, Scott knew Biff was right. The easiest thing to do *was* to turn back and go home.

He slipped out the old photo of his grandfather and gazed into the eyes of Shackleton Flipper. Shackleton had managed to cross this hard desolate terrain. Yes it was empty wilderness, but somewhere out here there might just be a place they could make their home. Once

First base camp: Scott yet to learn how to set the camera timer!

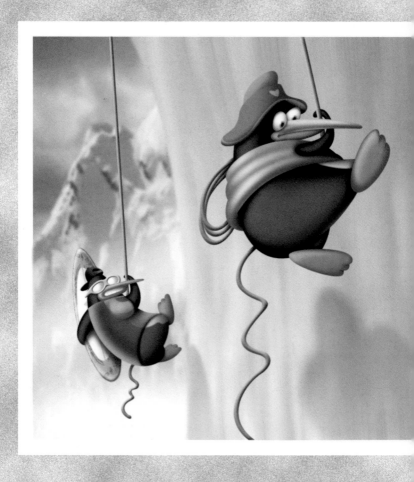

Humboldt's abseiling technique lets him down!

Penguin Expedition prepare to enter Canyon of Doom.

again it was as if the great explorer's spirit was reaching out to Scott from the past, banishing all his doubts. It was almost as if he could hear his grandfather's voice, a tiny whisper, echoing down the years. There was no mistaking what it was saying.

"The South Pole," said Scott.

"South Pole, here we come!" cheered Amelia, Dude and Humboldt.

"South Pole, here we come," muttered Biff and Brittany, and they sighed.

"Which way, Humboldt?" Scott asked.

"That way," Humboldt pointed. "Into the Zone of..." He tried to read what it said on Henson's map, "Zone of... It's smudged."

Scott looked at the map. He screwed up his eyes till he could read the words. "Zone of Certain Death," he said.

"Zone of Certain Death, here we come," Amelia mumbled, but no one cheered.

"It's just a name," said Humboldt. "Like 'greenhouse'. Everyone calls it greenhouse, but it's not green."

"Exactly," said Scott, "it's just a name..."

"Besides," said Humboldt, "in a wilderness like this..."

"Exactly," said Scott, "who'd be out in a wilderness like this?"

The penguins agreed that Scott and Humboldt

were right. However, unknown to them, across the empty wasteland strode Rocky Ice Berg. His heavy feet stamped on the ground, throwing up blasts of snow. There, under a thin covering, lay the remains of the penguins' last camp.

Ice squatted down and swept away the surface layer of snow with his flippers. Underneath, set hard in the frost, were six sets of small penguin footprints.

"Hur-hur-hur-hur," went Ice, and set out into the wilderness.

Just then, the penguins were plunging into the Zone of Certain Death. Ice wasn't far behind and he was coming their way.

Chapter Nineteen

In the morning, the skies were clear. It had stopped snowing and the wind had died down. Birds were flying again.

On a high crag of rock perched a young skua. He had dark feathers, a sharp beak and eager eyes. A second skua swooped overhead. He circled and landed on the same crag. He was bigger, with grizzled feathers and old cruel eyes.

The young skua squawked, "Dad, Dad, what d'you find on your food reconnaissance? What, huh, what?"

"Your dad's had hisself one very successful sortie," replied the old skua. "Oh yeah. Thirty miles north-north-east, I seen a rock, 'n' on it was one real juicy layer o' slime."

"Yuck! Not another winter of eating slime!"

The young skua peered at the empty wasteland. Snow stretched in every direction. He squinted. The wasteland wasn't empty, after all. Far far below, six black specks were trudging towards the opening of a tall rocky canyon. "Look, Dad, look!" cried the young skua. "Food!"

"What food? Where?"

"Down there! Penguins!"

"Penguins?" the old skua sneered. "This far from the sea? You tryin' to take the rise out your old dad, son? You gotta get up pretty early in the mornin', if you're gonna—" Then the old skua looked for himself. Six black specks *were* moving towards the walls of a huge canyon of snow and rock. "*Penguins*," he said. "Good spot, son – you got eagle eyes."

"Quick, Dad," squawked the young skua, already fluttering his wings to get airborne, "let's swoop down there now and eat one of 'em!"

"No, son," said the old skua, shaking his head. He crossed his wings on his breast. "This is 'bout air superiority. Penguins is birds like us, but they can't fly. Heck, they might as well be fish." The old skua chuckled until he coughed up slime and had to stop.

"Right, Dad."

"So we ain't gonna swoop down there now 'n' eat one of 'em. No, sir." The old skua pulled on a leather flying helmet and set a pair of goggles over his eyes. "We's gonna glide down there, 'n' eat 'em *all*."

Chapter Twenty

The penguins approached the opening of the tall rocky canyon. Snow spun in small whirlwinds, drifting into piles. The wind howled, loosening chips that plummeted from the sheer sides.

"Wow," said Dude, "this is, like, spectacular."

"Let's take a rest for a minute," Scott ordered.

The penguins laid down their rucksacks and massaged their weary muscles. Scott set up the camera and everyone posed in front of the canyon.

"Wait," Brittany squawked, "I'm not ready." She pulled out her compact and began to put on more make-up. Amelia huffed and puffed impatiently.

"I'm ready for my photograph now," Brittany announced at long last, and Scott snapped the picture.

Next the penguins had sips of drink and bites of food from their rations.

"Time's up," said Scott, hoisting his rucksack back onto his shoulder. "Let's move on."

The penguins trudged forwards. The canyon walls began to enclose them, plunging them into an eerie twilight.

"What's this place called?" Scott asked.

Humboldt studied the map. "I'm not sure," he said. "It's either the Gorge of Nice Things or the Canyon of Doom." The wind rushed through the canyon like the howling of a ghost. "Any guesses?"

The fall of rock chips became heavier. Some boulders shook loose from the high cliff walls and crashed down behind them. Snow and dust sprayed high into the air. When they settled, the penguins saw that the rocks had formed a wall that blocked any retreat.

"Up there!" Amelia shrieked. "*Who* is that?"

At the top of one of the canyon walls, far above them, a figure loomed. It was a big ugly penguin with thick tattooed flippers, and he was tossing down boulders as if they were no heavier than footballs.

"RUN!" shouted Scott, and the penguins scrambled across the canyon floor.

Ahead of them shone bright light. The canyon opened into a sunlit snowy plain. "Keep running!" Scott called. "We're going to get out!"

A rope plunged down the high cliff wall and Ice abseiled down to the ground, cutting off their escape.

The penguins skidded to a halt. Everyone looked at Scott.

He mumbled, "OK ... er ... nobody panic."

But, of course, a second later all the penguins were running in circles squawking, "We're going to die! We're going to die!"

"I think you can leave this to me," Biff declared. He faced Ice. "Berg, isn't it? Now see here, Berg, I'm Biff Beak and I command you to step aside."

Ice took a heavy step towards him.

Biff continued, "I'm quite sure that Boss Beak, *my dad*, wouldn't be very happy if he found out you'd been threatening his son and heir."

At this point, Ice grasped Biff's flipper and gave him the worst Chinese burn any of them had ever seen. Smoke billowed off his skin.

"Ow!" Biff yelped. "That smarts!"

"Biff, man, you smell like barbecue chicken," said Dude.

"Rub snow on it!" Brittany cried.

Scott spotted, high on the rock wall, a huge heavy boulder teetering directly above Ice. With

Biff and Brittany causing a distraction, he sneaked a catapult into his flippers.

Unfortunately Ice saw what he was up to.

Scott raised his flippers in surrender. "Let the others go," he said, his voice trembling. "I'm the leader of this expedition. It was all my idea."

Ice shrugged and, with a loud animal shriek, charged towards him.

Amelia snatched Brittany's compact.

"You can't use that!" Brittany wailed. "You don't have my bone structure!"

Amelia angled the mirror so it caught the sunlight streaming into the canyon and reflected the rays into Ice's eyes, momentarily blinding him.

Scott loaded a stone into his catapult and launched it skywards. The pebble struck the boulder which wobbled, shook loose and plummeted down onto Ice.

He took the full force of it on his great barrel breast. For a moment he teetered, then his eyes rolled back in his head and he toppled backwards into the snow with a thud that echoed up and down the canyon.

At first, the penguins were too shocked to move. Then Scott cried, "RUN!" and they scrambled past Ice's body and the boulder that lay on top of him like a big round tombstone, and charged out into the open plain beyond the canyon, to safety.

Later that day a gale began to blow. It howled through the canyon, pushing a drift of snow over Ice's body. His menacing eyes never blinked. His tattooed flippers and his short thick legs stayed still. The snowdrift rose higher and higher until, when night fell, it had buried Ice from view.

Chapter Twenty-one

The penguins didn't stop running till the canyon had fallen far behind them. By then it was dark. They threw down their rucksacks and collapsed on top of them, gasping for breath.

"Phew!" said Dude. "Am I glad to be out of that Gorge of Nice Things!"

Scott reached over with a flipper and patted Amelia's shoulder. "Thank you for saving my life," he murmured.

Amelia put her flipper round him and gave him a hug.

Scott was surprised. Nervously, he hugged her back. This was the moment he'd dreamed about – Amelia in his flippers at last. He told himself that she was just pleased he was safe, yet she wasn't letting go, as if she didn't ever want the hug to end.

Amelia had been so terrified that Ice would

hurt Scott. She'd had no time to think about it when it was happening, but now she wondered if she hadn't *just* been worried about the expedition losing its leader. Holding him in her flippers, she found herself imagining what it would be like if Scott wasn't around, when the expedition finished and everything returned to normal. That's why she was still clinging onto him – because she wanted to carry on being with him all day, every day. And she found herself hoping that maybe, just maybe, Scott was beginning to feel the same way about her...

"Guys," Dude squawked, "I don't want to ruin a truly beautiful moment, but I'm, like, freezing my flippers off here."

Scott let Amelia go. "Dude's right," he said. "The blizzard's closing in."

Amelia shuffled back, feeling very foolish. How silly she'd been to imagine Scott was thinking the same thing as her. All he cared about was the expedition. She blushed. She didn't dare look at him again.

Scott said, "Let's set up camp."

Wearily, the penguins hauled themselves up. They bent their backs into the wind and unfurled their tents. The canvasses flapped as they struggled to pitch them.

"You know, Scott," said Humboldt, "I never realized it was possible for the weather to be *too cold*." Not only had he buttoned up his anorak, he had also pulled his hat down over his earholes and slipped gloves onto the ends of his flippers. "What if, at the South Pole, it's like this all the time?"

Brittany packed snow round Biff's singed flipper, bandaged it and tied it up in a sling. He whispered, "Dad's plan to sabotage the expedition has failed. Now's my chance to show him what I'm capable of."

"Biff," Brittany whispered back, "that thug attacked *you* too. Why help your father, when he couldn't care less if you get hurt?"

"That's how he's got where he is today," Biff's voice was as cold and harsh as the blizzard building around them. "Nice penguins don't win. And I'm going to prove to my dad that I can be just as ruthless as he is."

Amelia opened the rucksacks of food supplies. Before she gave out the rations, she counted what was left. She felt cheered that there was enough food for at least another week – enough, just about, if anything went wrong, to get them home.

Soon afterwards, the penguins gobbled down their evening rations and zipped themselves into their tents to nest.

The night blackened. The blizzard blew. Snow piled up against the sides of the tents.

When he was sure everyone was asleep, Biff crawled out into the storm. Wincing as he bumped his sore flipper, he loosened the pegs holding each tent in place. Then he crawled back inside his tent and zipped it shut.

Moments later, a freezing draught of wind blasted snow into Scott's tent. The canvas toppled over and, though he stayed wrapped in his nesting bag, his head and flippers were now exposed to the blizzard. He blinked snow from his sleepy eyes. The wind was kicking all the tents along the ice. End over end, they were tumbling into the dark waste. Amelia, Dude, Humboldt, Biff and Brittany were struggling to get out of their nesting bags as the wind ripped the canvas off the food supplies and hurled them out into the night.

"OUR RATIONS!" Scott shrieked above the storm. "Grab the guy!"

"What guy?" said Dude. "There's only us here."

"The tent rope – it's called a 'guy'."

The guy snagged Amelia's flipper and started to drag her across the ice. Dude grabbed her, but the force of the wind pulled him along too.

Scott leapt out of his nesting bag and dived onto Dude's feet. With one flipper, he gripped a tent peg that was still fixed in the snow. With the other, he clung onto Dude, and Dude clung onto Amelia.

Humboldt spiralled up into the air, blown by a cyclone. He snatched at a tent pole and managed to grab its tip. He held on, squawking, as the blizzard spun him round like a weathercock.

Brittany's face was a mask of night cream. Snowflakes stuck to it, plastering her until her head resembled a giant snowball.

Pots and pans tore loose from their storage rack. The wind flung them at Biff. Clanging, they battered him about the head and body.

The penguins clung onto whatever their flippers could grasp. The snowstorm swirled all about them, getting thicker and thicker, till it drew across them like a curtain and they disappeared from view.

Chapter Twenty-two

Come morning, strong winds still raked across the wilderness, though the snow had stopped falling. It lay in heaps on what had once been the penguins' camp.

The heaps stirred. Scott surfaced first, shaking off clumps of frost. The first thing he did was check in his pocket for the photograph of his grandfather. It was still there, but damp around the edges.

Dude and Amelia emerged next, and Biff appeared, amid a pile of pots and pans, with lots of bruises to add to his burned flipper.

Then out of the snow rose a monster with a giant snowball for a head. The penguins scrambled away in fear. To everyone's relief, the "monster" clawed the snow from its head, revealing Brittany.

"Humboldt?" said Scott. "Where's Humboldt?"

He and Dude scraped snow off a strangely-shaped structure. Humboldt was frozen to the tent pole, his teeth chattering. They split the frost between his flippers and the pole, and stood him upright.

"The blizzard might only let up for a couple of hours," said Scott. "Let's find what stuff we can."

With the wind buffeting them, the shivering penguins clawed through the snow in search of their supplies.

Scott found some of his polar survival clothing.

Dude recovered a stick of dynamite. "Excellent!" he exclaimed.

Humboldt found a small cloth pouch. Inside it was a tiny magnet. He stared at it in puzzlement. Then he took out his compass and touched the magnet to its back. The needle started to spin wildly, just as it had when they'd been travelling in circles. "A *magnet*," he gasped. "That's why we kept going off course. The world acts like a big magnet to make the compass point north, but if you put even a little magnet nearby, it makes it point in the wrong direction."

"Excuses!" Biff cried.

"Yes," added Brittany. "I mean, who'd do a thing like that?"

"The same penguin who loosened the tent pegs," said Scott.

113

Shocked, all the others looked towards him. He was brandishing a tent peg he'd dug out of the snow. Caught in its hook was a thread of bright red wool. Scott had black gloves, Amelia yellow and Dude blue. Humboldt's gloves were light green with yellow flowers. Brittany's were brown. Biff's were *bright red*.

The penguins stared at Biff.

He started shuffling backwards. "I'm not saying a word without my lawyer present," he mumbled. "I'm a penguin. I don't belong in a kangaroo court."

Humboldt marched towards Biff. "You blamed *me* for getting us lost and all along it was *you*!" He charged at Biff with his flippers flailing, hurled snowballs that missed and then toppled over in a heap. "I never was any good at fighting," he moaned.

Scott helped him to his feet.

"Why, Biff?" Amelia demanded. "Why did you do this to us?"

"I only wanted to lose a couple of tents," Biff wailed, "just enough to make us turn back."

"Without our food supplies, it's not just the South Pole we won't reach," she replied. "We don't even stand a chance of making it *home*."

"Leave him alone!" Brittany squawked.

"Shut up, princess!" Amelia cried. "I've had just about enough of you, d'you hear me?" and she shoved Brittany over into a snowdrift.

Dude marched up to Biff and slapped him hard with his flipper. "We could, like, *die* out here, man," he growled, towering over him.

"Hit him again!" Humboldt squawked.

Dude punched Biff in the belly.

Biff's belly wobbled and he doubled over in pain. He gasped, "How was I supposed to know the storm would blow the food away?"

"You've put your precious inheritance above our lives and the lives of every penguin in Penguinville," Amelia snarled.

"It wasn't about money!" Biff sobbed.

"Oh no?" said Amelia in disbelief, folding her flippers across her breast.

"So what was it, jerk?" Dude demanded.

"Hit him again!" Humboldt squawked.

Dude slapped Biff on the beak.

Biff's head still stung where Dude had hit him the first time. Now he rubbed his bruised beak with his good flipper. "It was all to prove my dad wrong," he said. "To stop him hating me ... and start loving me."

Biff started sobbing. "It's only fair if you want to punish me now," he croaked.

"Hit him again!" Humboldt squawked.

Dude looked at Scott. "Should I?" he asked. "Or maybe I should whack him with a shovel?"

Scott shook his head and waved Dude away.

He patted Biff on the shoulder. "Your dad treats all the penguins so badly," he said, "that I suppose none of us ever stopped to wonder how he treated you. There won't be any punishment, Biff. You've had enough already."

Scott gave him a hug, but that only made Biff cry even harder.

Amelia unfolded her flippers and patted Biff on the back. "There, there," she said. "You let it all out."

Dude frowned. "You sure about this, guys? You know, maybe I should get the shovel…"

"Hit him again!" Humboldt squawked.

From above came a piercing high-pitched shriek. The penguins looked up. A pair of skuas were circling overhead.

"Contact!" squawked the old skua. "Two o'clock, low! Look at 'em now, son. They's tired 'n' cold 'n' arguin' 'tween theirselves. They's easy pickin's for you 'n' your old dad, yes sir! You be my wing man, son. Get in tight – echelon formation. We's goin' in!"

"Roger!" the young skua squawked back.

The skuas swooped down towards the penguins. The penguins covered their heads with their flippers and ran for cover.

"Duck!" Scott cried.

"I don't think they're ducks, man," said Dude. "They look more like skuas."

The old skua swooped low and hooked Amelia in his beak. Amelia tried to flap him away. "DUDE, HELP ME!" she shrieked. "DUDE!"

The young skua clasped one of her flippers and together they plucked her into the air.

Dude sprinted after them.

With every beat of their wings, the skuas lifted Amelia from the ground, but then sank back before the next beat.

Dude made a diving tackle.

The skuas flapped hard and rose higher. Dude's outstretched flippers brushed their talons, but they climbed higher still, and Dude crashed back to Earth.

"DUDE!" Amelia shrieked, but he was skidding helplessly across the ice. Then he smashed into a snowdrift.

"Yee-hah!" the old skua squawked. "Fifty feet 'n' climbin'!"

Down on the ground, Scott packed snow into a hard ball.

Humboldt passed him the catapult. "Range, twenty metres; elevation, forty-five degrees," he judged.

Scott took aim and launched the snowball.

Amelia struggled to break free, but the ground was falling further and further below as the skuas soared away.

"Such a lovely tender juicy penguin!" the young one cried. "She's going to taste so good in a light slime sauce with—"

The snowball splattered the young skua. Snow pasted his feathers. "There's bogeys all over me!" he squawked. The snow was in his wings and he was looping out of control. "I'm in a flat spin heading out to snow!"

The young skua collided with his dad, knocking Amelia out of his beak. Then they both spiralled off into the distance and crashed to the ground, throwing up a plume of snow.

As Amelia plunged back to Earth, she shrieked in terror. She flapped her wings madly in an effort to fly but, of course, it made no difference.

Scott scrambled across the ice to catch her. She crashed into him and the two of them tumbled, beak over tail feathers, into the same snowdrift as Dude.

Humboldt, Biff and Brittany ran across the ice and began to claw at the snow. They pulled Dude out first. Then they dug out Scott and Amelia, who coughed and spat out snow.

"They're alive!" Humboldt cried.

Scott felt his beak and flippers. They were bruised, but nothing was broken.

Amelia wiped snow from her face. She blinked at Scott. "My hero," she said.

Chapter Twenty-three

The penguins huddled together. The search for supplies was over. What little they could find, they had collected into a pile. There were a few items of clothing and a bottle of water. All the food was gone. Their tents had been carried away by the wind. Now the snow had started falling again and the wind was gusting hard, chilling them to their wishbones. They shivered. Their teeth chattered. Their beaks and flippers turned blue.

"It's too cold," Humboldt wailed. "I never thought I'd say it, but it's *too cold*."

Dude moaned, "Man, what I wouldn't give right now to be back in Penguinville Bay, soakin' up some rays."

Snow peppered Scott's goggles. He peered up into the sky and, through the blizzard, caught a fleeting glimpse of enormous beating wings.

"The albatrosses," he murmured, and then he realized where they were going.

Moments later, Scott was securing his goggles, gloves, hat and walking poles. "When the albatrosses migrate," he explained to the others, "this is their flight path. I thought Henson was just raving – he kept saying, 'The albatross, the albatross.' But Base Camp Albatross – it's got to be *here* somewhere. I'm guessing it'll have food supplies. They'll be frozen but, even after all these years, they'll be usable. I'm going to follow the albatrosses' flight path. If I'm right, I'll find my grandpa's supplies and bring them back before nightfall."

"I'll come," Dude said.

"Me too," said Humboldt.

"No," said Scott, "I'm the explorer. Sorry, but you'll only slow me down. I'm going out now. I may be some time." He turned to go.

Amelia grabbed his flipper. "Scott ... be careful," she said.

He nodded. "I'll be back."

Then he strode away. In a matter of seconds, he had disappeared into the blizzard.

Chapter Twenty-four

Scott trudged over the frozen ground. Snow-flakes plastered his puffa jacket. The wind whipped his eyes and the tip of his beak. He leaned into the storm, straining every muscle and sinew, gasping for breath, pushing to the very limit of his endurance.

An object poked out of the ice. Scott had been hiking for what seemed like hours when he stumbled over it. He wiped his goggles and scraped frost off the object. It appeared to be a glove. He tugged on the glove and it came off in his hand, leaving a frozen flippertip sticking out of the ice.

Scott scraped round the flipper until he had taken off the top crust of snow. Buried beneath the ice, deep-frozen perhaps for centuries or longer, was some kind of creature.

Just as he was about to wipe off the frost that

covered the creature's face, Scott was struck in the back by something heavy. He rolled across the ice, wrestling with his attacker.

"Scott! Scott! Stop it! It's me!"

"Biff?" said Scott. "What are you doing here? I told you to wait for me."

"But I wanted to help. It's my fault we're in this mess."

Scott sighed. "Now you're here, I suppose you could help me dig."

Together they hacked the frozen creature out of the ice, clawing hunks of frost off its body. Soon only a thin coat of ice remained, through which they could make out seal fur.

"It's some sort of deformed seal!" cried Biff.

They scraped away more ice to reveal tweeds and hobnailed boots.

"No it's not," Scott realized. "It's a penguin!"

In one flipper, the penguin was holding a quill, in the other, a journal. As the frost crystals melted away, Scott read from the journal,

"Had I lived, I should have had a tale to tell of hardihood, endurance and courage, which would have stirred the heart of every penguin. These rough notes and my dead—"

The frozen penguin's eyes blinked open. Frosty scales fell from its eyes and beak. "—my dead body must tell the tale," it croaked.

Biff jumped and crashed back onto the ice. "It's alive!" he squealed.

Scott stared into the face of the defrosted penguin. He knew the beard and the half-moon spectacles before him. It was like staring at a ghost. "Grandpa!" he cried, and flung his flippers round Shackleton.

"What?" gasped Biff. "This is *Shackleton Flipper*?"

"It certainly is!" Scott replied. "Grandpa, I can't believe it's you. All my life I've wished I could meet you!"

"Steady on there, lad," the defrosted penguin commanded. "Shackleton Flipper I may be, but I'm no one's grandpa. I do have a son. Always talking about being a schoolmaster. But he's barely older than you."

"Your son is *my dad*," Scott exclaimed.

Shackleton looked confused.

"I'll have to explain everything later," said Scott. "We're running out of time. Can you lead us to Base Camp Albatross?"

Shackleton grinned, causing icicles to splinter off his beard. "They don't call me the greatest explorer in penguin history for nothing," he said.

He unbuttoned a cord from his tweed jacket.

He tugged on it and a guy lifted out of the snow, frozen hard after all these years. It stretched ahead. "Follow me, lads," Shackleton ordered, and struck out into the blizzard.

Scott and Biff shambled after the old explorer.

Scott gazed at his grandfather as he ploughed through the blizzard. He couldn't believe it. The man whose spirit had guided him through the wilderness had come back to life – and here he was, saving the expedition! Scott's weary trudges turned to skips of joy.

Chapter Twenty-five

Amelia, Dude, Humboldt and Brittany huddled together. Frost jewelled their faces and plastered their feathers. Their beaks chattered and they were white as statues.

"You know, this is gettin' kinda grim," Dude murmured.

"Maybe Scott's not going to make it back, after all?" said Humboldt. "Maybe we're not going to make it back home, either…"

Brittany sobbed, "Biff told me his plan to sabotage the expedition, but I didn't stop him. If we get out of this alive, I promise I'll never ever do a bad deed again."

"It's too late to feel guilty," said Amelia. "I forgive you. I'm sorry for all the fights we've had. Let's at least end things as friends."

Brittany and Amelia hugged each other, and started to cry. Soon Humboldt was sobbing too.

Even Dude had to sniff back tears. "Amelia," he said, "since we're all getting stuff off our breasts ... I gotta tell you this now, 'cause I might never get another chance. You know the poem I wrote for you – well, it wasn't actually, er, me. It was Scott. He did it. Guess he had kind of a crush on you all along, babe."

It was the news Amelia longed to hear – Scott felt for her as she did for him. But it had come too late and she wept bitterly. "Scott," she sighed.

"And Biff," said Brittany. "Poor guys, they're alone out there. At least when the time comes, we've got each other."

Shapes appeared in the blizzard. Snow drew over them, then cleared again. The penguins peered hard into the whiteness. Perhaps they had only imagined what they'd seen? Then the wind blew the snow clear again and there, hefting lifesaving supplies, were Scott, Biff and Shackleton.

"Scott," Amelia murmured, and this time she wept with relief.

Chapter Twenty-six

The gale breathed its last. The snow stopped falling. The skies cleared. Under a starlit night, the penguins broke out their new supplies.

From a battered leather haversack, Shackleton distributed tins of fish, originally preserved in brine but now frozen solid. "We even carried a fishbowl so that we could keep some alive for greater freshness," he remarked, "though it appears lost from these supplies."

From deep inside another sack, Shackleton produced a store of kindling and firewood, still dry after all these years. He built a fire, over which he defrosted the fish.

Then, ringed by antique canvas tents, the penguins ate and warmed themselves round the glowing campfire.

Soon Shackleton Flipper was pouring everyone hot coffee from a vintage flask. "Tell me this, Scott, lad," he asked, "what inspired this journey of exploration that you and your brave young band have undertaken?"

"Grandpa, Penguinville is melting. Years of pollution are ruining the environment. The climate's changing."

"Surely though, the townspenguins will stop the pollution?" Shackleton said.

"The grown-ups don't care," Amelia said bitterly. "All they care about is having a comfortable life *today*. They don't want to worry about what things'll be like in the *future*."

"How foolish they are," Shackleton murmured, "for they do not understand that what we do to the Earth, we do to our children."

The young penguins hung their beaks in sadness.

Scott sipped from his beaker of coffee and said, "Grandpa, tell us about your expedition."

"For years," Shackleton began, "I dreamt that I would one day be the first penguin ever to stand upon that most particular spot, the very bottom of the world – the South Pole. Twelve of us set out from Penguinville. We encountered much hardship and many were forced to turn back in defeat. But I would not surrender, nor would my faithful colleague, Henson. Aye, the South Pole proved she would forever remain a pitiless adversary, for on that final day she

128

brought upon us the blizzard to end all blizzards. Frostbite had taken hold of Henson's flippertips, so I ordered him to remain behind while I made the final push for the Pole. That very blizzard froze me, young friends, as I entered in my journal the words I believed would prove my last, prior to interment in that chillsome grave."

"So did you get there, or not?" asked Humboldt.

"Where?" said Shackleton.

"The South Pole, of course," Scott put in.

"Why Scott, lad," Shackleton answered, "in all honesty, I don't know."

"When you froze, you were on your way back, weren't you?" Scott stared intently at his grandfather.

Shackleton shifted uncomfortably. "Truth be told, lad, my bearings were somewhat confounded by the abominable conditions. Unsure of my precise position, I planted a flag. Where it truly lies – upon the Pole, or a distance short – I confess I know not."

"But Grandpa," Scott gulped, "I've always believed that you ... that you reached the South Pole."

"I can't say for sure that I did," Shackleton admitted. "I'm sorry."

Scott moaned, "So you can't tell us if we

could live there?"

"*Live* there? Why should any penguin wish to do that?"

"It's the entire reason for our expedition!" Scott wailed. He buried his face in his flippers.

Shackleton's eyes darted to the others in confusion.

Humboldt explained, "You see, sir, we thought, with the warmer climate, the best place to live would be the South Pole."

Shackleton reached out and laid a flipper round Scott's shoulders. He spoke quietly and gravely. "This is a place of unimaginable hardship. It is a lifeless inhospitable wilderness and no penguin, not even ones as brave and resolute as you have proved yourselves, could live off this desolate land. Lad, it breaks my heart to say so, but your trek has been in vain."

Scott couldn't bear to hear any more. He leapt to his feet and scuttled to the edge of the camp. Amelia and Humboldt rose to follow him, but Shackleton wagged a flipper for them to stay where they were.

"Leave the lad," he advised. "Leave him to his private reflections."

Alone, Scott stared into the distance. He felt utter despair. Everything, this whole expedition, had been for nothing.

The eerie coloured lights of the aurora

australis shimmered across the clear black sky. Scott squatted with his flippers on his lap, his shoulders hunched. He could hear the others getting into their tents and nesting down for the night. In the end, only Amelia was left. She padded out to the edge of the camp and squatted beside him.

"They're beautiful," she said, pointing up to the aurora's rainbow of lights. "Humboldt explained what they are. They're tiny particles from the sun interacting with a part of the atmosphere called the, er, the…"

"The ionosphere," said Scott.

"That's right. That's what Humboldt called it." She laid a flipper on his shoulder. "At least you found your grandpa. That's one good thing that's come out of this expedition."

Scott took out the old photo of Shackleton. "He was like a guardian angel watching over me. He was a voice in my head saying, 'You can do it. *I* made it. So can you. Go on.' But now that he's here, he's stopped being a legend. He's an ordinary penguin who doubts he made it to the South Pole at all. And what's worse, he doesn't believe we could ever live there."

"When you grow up," Amelia said, "there comes a time when there isn't someone else's trail to follow any more. You've got to make a new one of your own. For you and for all of us,

131

Scott, that time is now. How can we know for sure the South Pole *won't* be a place for penguins to live, unless we see for ourselves?" She pointed out into the snowy wastes. "I get the feeling that the South Pole can't be all that far from here. It's time to finish the job we started."

Scott peered out into the icy wilderness that gleamed like ivory under the starlight and under the lights of the aurora, and he knew that she was right. In the morning, they must make the final push for the South Pole.

He turned to look at her, and her beak was right next to his. "Time to finish the job we started," he said.

She smiled and they kissed each other for the first time.

Chapter Twenty-seven

In a canyon far behind the penguins, the wind was skimming layers of snow off a snowdrift. Gradually it blew the coverings off a short stout figure pinned under a rock. Soon the figure's head was revealed. Its eyes were open and staring. Then a muscle twitched. Eyes blinked.

Any normal penguin would have been groggy after being unconscious for so long. But not Ice Berg. He strained every muscle and with a gigantic effort rolled the boulder off his breast. His joints creaked and clumps of snow crumbled from his feathers. He stood up, scanning the vast terrain that lay like an enormous white blanket under the clear starlit night.

Ice opened his backpack. From his supplies, he bit off a piece of frozen seal meat. Then, from the bottom of the pack, he produced a clutch of dynamite sticks.

"Hur-hur-hur-hur," he went.

Then he bounded out of the canyon, once more on the trail of the penguins.

Chapter Twenty-eight

The landscape was white and empty apart from seven dark specks crossing the ice towards the south. The ground rose ahead of them as the penguins bent into their journey, heaving their equipment uphill.

Clouds covered the sky, dropping a gentle snowfall. The wind was pleasantly chill.

"This is penguin weather," said Amelia, and smiled at Scott.

"Definitely is," he answered. "Just perfect." He smiled back at her.

Just then Dude looked round and Scott wiped the grin from his beak.

Amelia did the same. Her heart pounded. That first time at the beach, with his blond feathers and white smile and big muscles, Dude had seemed like her dream penguin. How could she tell him that she had fallen in love with Scott?

"The conditions are clement indeed," Shackleton remarked for all to hear. "My memory of that journey of thirty years ago is of weather that was considerably harsher."

"Then it might be true, after all?" Humboldt interrupted. "True, I mean, sir, that the climate change has affected the South Pole too. While it's made Penguinville too hot for penguin life, the South Pole has warmed up to become just right for us."

"Perhaps," Shackleton answered.

At the top of the hill, the ice began to flatten out. The old penguin paused for a moment. He scanned the empty wastes. Not a bird swooped in the sky. No living thing crawled over the land. All was silent apart from the gusting wind.

Shackleton's eyes met Scott's. "But a pleasant wilderness is a wilderness all the same," he said. "No home for a penguin."

Scott nodded gravely.

Shackleton turned to move on, but almost at once came to a halt. The far side of the hill fell away steeply. It plunged down and down into a gigantic ravine that stretched as far as the eye could see. The penguins stood atop a sheer cliff of ice that was higher and steeper than even the biggest cliffs of Penguinville Bay. It was as if a giant had gouged a trench out of the landscape.

"This is the end," said Biff sadly. "We've come so far and now…" His voice trailed off. He sniffed and wiped his beak. The penguin who'd set out to sabotage the expedition was as disappointed as any of them that it now appeared certain to fail.

"But – but – the *map*—" Humboldt stammered. He unfolded Henson's chart for them all to see. "There's no ravine shown on here. It's not my fault."

"Not your fault, nor Henson's," said Shackleton. "I can declare with certainty that this great chasm was not present when we trekked this way all those years ago. It appears to be true that the South Pole's climate has changed for the better, only, to our deep misfortune, to have caused the formation of this impassable obstacle."

Silence fell on them all. They peered into the ravine. It was so deep that clouds had formed in its lower reaches.

Amelia sobbed. Brittany slumped down in the snow in defeat. Biff and Dude threw off their rucksacks in dismay. Humboldt tore up Henson's map and let the pieces flutter down into the ravine.

"Let us not dwell on our failure," said Shackleton. "We must make plans for the return journey to Penguinville."

137

"No," said Scott, digging his feet into the snow. "No."

The others turned to look at him.

"Grandpa, I love you, but you're wrong. That's the way the grown-ups back home think – and that's why they're sitting around doing nothing, while Penguinville melts into the sea. You see, I don't believe there's any such thing as an obstacle that can't be overcome."

Scott's voice fell into the ravine and there was complete silence, but a moment later it echoed back, "– *overcome.*"

Amelia struggled to her feet. "Nor me," she said. She pulled Brittany to her feet.

"Me too," Brittany said.

"Me too, man," said Dude, and hoisted his rucksack back onto his massive shoulders.

"Us too," said Humboldt and Biff together.

"Right then," Scott rallied them. "This is what we'll do. First we'll—"

Just then came a hissing sound. Scott spun round to see sticks of dynamite streaking across the snowy wastes towards them. The dynamite struck the ice and, a split second later, exploded, flinging up plumes of snow.

Cracks began opening all over the cliff. The penguins of the penguin expedition toppled over and clung to the ground as it quaked beneath their feet.

"What's happening?" Amelia shrieked.

"Some kind of ice quake!" Humboldt shrieked back.

"This is no ice quake!" Scott bellowed. "There's only one thing it can be!"

He scanned the terrain for the stout muscular figure of Ice Berg. Could he glimpse him far away through the curtain of falling snow? Could he hear his distant laugh going "Hur-hur-hur-hur" despite the creaking and rupturing of the ground beneath their feet?

There was no time to find out. Cracks were starting to shatter the ice shelf. Thick layers of snow were crumbling into enormous clouds of powder that fluttered down into the ravine. The shelf was collapsing in on itself.

"RUN!" Scott cried, and the penguins scrambled away from the widening ravine. They struggled to haul the equipment sledge behind them. It flipped over and a tent toppled out. Dude turned to chase the tent, but Scott shouted, "Leave it! Keep going!"

The ravine had deepened to double its size. All around the penguins, the ice shelf was giving way. Soon they'd fall to their deaths.

"What now?" Amelia gasped.

All eyes probed Scott.

Scott looked at Shackleton.

Shackleton said nothing, not knowing

what to do.

The ravine swallowed the ice beneath the lost tent. As it fell, Scott saw it fill out like a parachute. It fluttered in the air, rose for a couple of seconds and then began a gentle descent into the ravine.

Suddenly Scott had an idea. "Dude, break out the tents!" he ordered.

Shackleton realized at once what Scott was thinking and cried, "Good lad!"

"Amelia, Humboldt, Brittany," Scott said, "spread the tents flat and tie the canvasses together. Biff and Grandpa, help me make a frame out of the tent poles. Let's do it!"

Racing against time, Scott, Biff and Shackleton used climbing ropes to bind the tent poles and hiking poles into a frame, while the others tied the canvasses into a covering.

All the time, Scott peered over his shoulder, looking for Ice Berg. He wasn't dead, after all. He was lurking somewhere out in the wilderness – Scott was sure of it.

At the bottom of the equipment sledge, Dude found his surfboard. He'd forgotten he'd even brought it.

"You've been lugging a surfboard all the way to the South Pole?" Biff snorted.

"The dudester goes *nowhere* without his board."

"We'll use it as part of the frame," said Scott.

Dude helped fix the surfboard into place. "Man, this really really hurts," he muttered.

The ravine continued to expand. Pieces of the ice shelf were collapsing all around the penguins. The danger was creeping closer.

"There's not enough time!" Amelia squawked.

Scott asked, "Dude, d'you still have that dynamite?"

"Sure do, man," Dude replied and pulled it off the sledge.

"We'll use an explosion to try and seal ourselves off from the ravine," Scott told them.

"Explosions are so *cool*," said Dude. "I'll do it."

"No I will," said Scott, reaching for the dynamite.

"Yurghhh, I will, dude," said Dude, pushing Scott away.

"Listen, Dude," said Humboldt, "you've got to plant the dynamite on the line of expansion of the ravine, positioned so that, when the ice explodes, the ravine will deviate at least ninety degrees, and give yourself enough time to get away, bearing in mind a fuse delay of eight seconds. Got it?"

"Er ... no," said Dude.

Scott snatched the dynamite out of Dude's flipper and charged towards the ravine. He

141

leapt to the edge of the ice and planted the stick of dynamite. He packed snow round it, lit the fuse and scrambled away.

The dynamite exploded. Snow showered high into the air. The explosion cracked like thunder across the snowy wastes, shaking the ground beneath the penguins' feet. When the snow cleared, they saw that the ravine was now snaking away from them and Scott was running back to safety.

"He did it!" Dude cried.

Meanwhile, the others fixed the last strut and stretched the canvas over the frame of poles, forming a big balloon and passenger basket.

"Hold her down while I light the fire," said Shackleton.

Amelia, Humboldt, Brittany and Shackleton clambered into the basket. Dude and Biff planted their feet in the snow and clung fast to the rickety frame. Shackleton built a fire from his supply of wood and tinder, while Scott scrambled across the ice to join them.

Shackleton lit the flame. Hot air rose into the balloon and, slowly but surely, the canvas began to fill out.

But just then, the ice ruptured and a deep gorge cracked open between Scott and the others.

"SCOTT!" Amelia cried.

Scott peered down into the cavernous void.

He looked across at Amelia. "GO!" he shrieked. The snow began to break up beneath his feet. Scott turned and ran to harder ground, away from the hot-air balloon.

"Scott," Amelia wept.

He turned back one last time, tears streaming down his face. "GO!" he commanded. "Save yourselves."

"Scott, I'm sorry," Amelia sobbed.

Dude and Biff heaved the basket forward, and it started to gather speed as it skidded down towards the edge of the ravine. They leapt aboard just as the ice beneath them powdered away to nothing.

The penguins screamed as the balloon plunged down into the void. They threw more wood on the fire and fanned the flames with their flippers.

Moments later, the balloon soared out of the ravine and into the sky.

"I'm flying!" Amelia squawked. "I'm *flying*!"

The penguins peered down. As the ravine grew larger, a valley was being gouged out of the land. Scott stood atop the last pillar of ice.

Shackleton looked at his grandson. "Great God," he cried, "this is an awful place."

Amelia sobbed as she piloted the balloon.

Dude hugged her.

"Dude," she croaked, "I was working out

how I'd tell you … I love Scott."

Dude's beak fell open. He gazed into Amelia's eyes and then down at the shrinking figure of Scott, far below, about to be swallowed up into the crumbling ice.

He sighed, "I just hope I live to regret this." Then he ripped his surfboard from the basket.

Shocked, Humboldt grabbed at the loose ends and clasped them together.

"Meet me on the far side of the ravine!" Dude called, and then he leapt out of the basket on his surfboard.

Surfing the wind, Dude plummeted down towards the ice. Air rushed past him, folding back his blond feathers into a plume.

"Yee-hah!" he shrieked, bending his knees to keep the board flat and sticking out his flippers to balance himself upright. He crash-landed near Scott, but righted himself and scooped Scott onto his board.

Wobbling, squawking, the two of them careered off the edge of the ice and out into the great white void.

Amelia guided the hot-air balloon down towards them. As it swept past, Dude and Scott grabbed the bottom of the basket. The surfboard tumbled end over end for what seemed like an age, before hitting the floor of the valley below.

The balloon skimmed low over the ice. Scott and Dude began moving, flipper over flipper, up the side of the basket. Biff, Humboldt, Brittany and Shackleton reached over to help them aboard.

Something struck the bottom of the basket. The whole frame shuddered.

Amelia called, "We just picked up something big. Very big."

"Ice Berg!" cried Scott. "I knew it was him!"

A tattooed flipper began slashing through the floor of the basket.

"He's alive!" Humboldt screeched.

Shackleton tried to kick Ice away, but he was no match for the security chief's strength, and Ice began clambering aboard.

Still clinging onto the sides, Scott and Dude were powerless. "Grandpa!" Scott wailed.

Biff and Brittany leapt to the assistance of Shackleton and Humboldt. All four of them grasped Ice's flippers and struggled to peel them off the basket floor.

Ice glared up through the hole, growling, kicking at them with his powerful legs.

Biff and Brittany pulled and pulled until one of Ice's flippers was forced off the floor. A moment later, Shackleton kicked the other one away with his hobnailed boot.

There was only time for them to glimpse the

look of utter panic on Ice's previously emotionless face, before he bombed to the ground far below and disappeared forever into the white void.

Shackleton, Biff and Brittany helped Scott and Dude climb over the sides.

"We did it, guys!" Humboldt beamed.

"Scott, lad," said Shackleton, "you've made this explorer very proud."

The balloon soared aloft into a clear tranquil sky. The new ice valley fell behind them, and they glided out over solid ground again.

Scott shook Dude's flipper. "You saved my life," he murmured. "You could've got yourself killed. I'm so glad you didn't."

"It ain't all good news for the dudester," said Dude.

Scott glanced over at Amelia. "Amelia's told you?" he asked.

"Worse than that, man. I, like, lost my board."

Scott tottered to the other side of the basket. Amelia was weeping. He leaned towards her and kissed her.

"Oh go ahead, guys," Dude shrugged. "I guess the best penguin won." The basket swayed. "Whoa! But keep your eyes on the flying, dudes."

Chapter Twenty-nine

The balloon swooped south, towards the Pole.

Scott spotted something far ahead. "Binoculars," he ordered. Humboldt passed them over and Scott peered through them into the distance. He refocused the lenses just to make sure he wasn't seeing things.

"Scott...?" Humboldt enquired.

Scott mumbled, "Water ... birds ... fish..."

"Impossible, lad," Shackleton declared. "Your imagination is creating a *mirage* – a picture of what you *wish* to see." He snatched the binoculars from Scott.

But before he could take a look, Amelia shrieked, "We're losing height! We're going in!"

The fire burned the last piece of wood and the balloon descended. Amelia lined up on the ice as best she could and the basket skidded and bounced and skidded again. The penguins clung to its rickety frame, squawking in terror, as pieces broke off and clunked them on their heads and bodies. The basket skidded round on its side and juddered across the ice. Snow sprayed over the sides, plastering the penguins. Then the skidding stopped and the basket was at rest.

"Everyone OK?" Amelia shouted.

The others muttered and dusted themselves off, but no one was hurt.

"Thank you for flying Penguin Airways," said Amelia.

The penguins stumbled out of the basket and gathered in the now limp balloon.

One by one, they raised their eyes to scan their surroundings. One by one, their beaks fell open.

"This is no mirage," said Scott.

A lake of clear blue water rippled under a sky of fluffy clouds. The lake teemed with fish. Birds swooped and sang overhead.

"But ... but, how can this be?" Shackleton demanded.

At the edge of the lake, Humboldt found a weathered fishbowl. "I believe this is your answer, sir." He lifted it up to the light. On its side were the words SHACKLETON EXPEDITION.

"You said you brought live fish with you?"

"That's right, lad."

"When the climate started to warm up, they must have defrosted. That explains the lake too. Snow melted and filled a natural basin with water. The fish thrived, getting more numerous with every passing month. And the birds—"

"The birds can live here," Amelia interrupted, "because they feed on the fish. And if birds can live here—"

Scott finished for her, "Then so can *we*."

"OK," said Biff. "I get the lake, the fish and the birds. But what's that?" He pointed across the lake at an object flapping in the breeze.

Scott first, then Shackleton, the penguins began to trudge towards it.

"Where are we?" Scott whispered to Humboldt.

Humboldt pulled his sextant out of his rucksack.

As they got closer, they could make out a flag, battered with age, but still showing penguin markings.

Humboldt took a reading from the sextant. "Eighty-eight, eighty-nine, ninety ... *ninety degrees south*!"

"Good Lord," Shackleton gasped. "The South Pole!"

Scott pointed at the flag. "There it is, Grandpa. Look for yourself."

Shackleton scuttled up to the flag pole. He

touched the weathered banner and rubbed it between his flippertips. "My flag," he said.

"You did it, Grandpa," Scott murmured. "You *did* make it to the South Pole, after all."

"And so did you!" Shackleton grinned.

Scott and Shackleton, the two explorers, flung themselves into each other's flippers.

"The South Pole," said Dude. "Man, who'd've thought it?"

"Brr," said Amelia, "and it's lovely and cold."

Chapter Thirty

On the coast of Antarctica, once one of the coldest places on Earth, the sun was blazing more brightly than ever.

The birds had flown in search of shade. The whales had swum away to find cooler waters. All the fish had long been sucked up by the factory pipeline. The beach of Penguinville Bay was empty of penguins. The café had long since melted. Only the leopard seals remained, crowding the beach, mouths open, razor teeth gleaming in the sun. They had eaten any penguins that had strayed into the water to cool down and now the rest stayed away. But when the ice shelf collapsed, and that would be any day now, the seals knew they'd have a whole colony to feast on.

In the town that had once risen up from the great ice shelf and been home to a thousand penguin families, the igloos had flattened to sludge. The chimney of the Beak Corporation factory had melted. Workers were rebuilding it with whatever materials they could find – still following the orders of Boss Beak, still believing him when he told them that the heatwave would end soon.

The fish supply had run out, but Boss Beak assured the penguins that a new, even more powerful pipeline would soon be catching more.

Out of the pipes and machines of the production line, pollution still billowed up into the air to form a choking black cloud that squatted over the sweltering melting dying town.

The town square was a sinking lake of slush. Principal Flipper was leading a memorial service, attended by a host of townspenguins. Everyone was either dabbing tears from their eyes or sweat from their feathers.

Principal Flipper fought a quiver in his voice as he addressed the crowd. "They set out to save their community—"

"If only we'd listened," wailed Amelia's mother, and began to sob. "Now we're all going to be eaten by seals."

"They set out to save their community," continued Principal Flipper, "and now, after so long without word, we must presume them lost forever, their young lives snatched away."

"They're gone," wailed Henson. "Just like Shackleton. It's all my fault again." He gulped from his bottle and swayed.

"And so, today," Principal Flipper went on, "we honour their memory." A band struck up a dirge. Mourners laid wreaths at a memorial that was already half melted. "Scott – my own son. Humboldt. Amelia. Quentin – known to everyone as 'Dude'. Biff. Brittany."

There were mutterings in the crowd.

Principal Flipper coughed loudly. "Ladies and gentlemen, please," he said, "show some respect on this solemn occasion."

The mutterings grew louder. Principal Flipper glanced up angrily. Heads were turning towards the edge of the town square. Penguins were jostling each other for a view of seven weary figures who were staggering up the main street, dragging a sledge. Some started shouting and the seven weary figures stumbled to a halt. Principal Flipper put on his glasses and squinted at them.

"Scott!" he cried and ran through the crowd towards his son. Then, as he got closer, he noticed the tall bearded penguin with them and gasped, "Dad?"

Shackleton studied the middle-aged penguin waddling towards him. "Son?" he said.

Henson looked at the returning children and

saw among them the bearded figure from the past. *"Shackleton?"*

Shackleton peered at the grizzled old penguin. *"Henson?"*

Henson wept. "I thought you were dead. I thought it was all my fault." Then he tossed his bottle into the slush, never to reach for it again.

Scott and his father and Shackleton and Henson all hugged. Amelia's parents threw their flippers round her. Her girlfriends started telling Dude how much they'd missed seeing him at the beach. Brittany's mum and dad kissed her and welcomed Biff back from the dead. Humboldt searched the crowd. A motorized wheelchair slid through the slush towards him.

"Dad!" Humboldt cried.

"Son!" cried Doctor Frost.

"Dad, I'm sorry but we proved you wrong."

Doctor Frost gave Humboldt a playful tip on the beak. "You?" he grinned.

Scott called for attention. "Everyone, listen! Listen! We reached the South Po—"

Before he could finish, a puff of cigar smoke was blown in his face. He coughed and rubbed his eyes.

Boss Beak shoved Scott aside and the crowd fell silent. He took the cigar from his beak and thundered, *"I* still decide what we build and where! The heatwave is going to end soon and the Beak Corporation will begin a programme of reconstruction. A new Penguinville will rise out of the slush. But it will still be *my* Penguinville."

"And you'll build a new factory, won't you, Dad?" said Biff.

"That's right," said Boss Beak. "At last, boy, you're talking like a businessman."

"A new factory that'll kill all the fish and create more pollution and ruin the environment all over again," said Biff.

The crowd murmured in support of Biff.

"Silence, boy!" roared Boss Beak.

"No. You never listen to anything I say. And I don't care anymore – because I've got new friends and between us we made the penguin expedition a success!"

Boss Beak shook with rage. "Ignore these children. Every penguin, do as I command! Return to your work at once!"

Shackleton pushed through the crowd towards Boss Beak. He strode straight up to him and squawked, "You haven't changed much, have you? Even when you were a boy, you were a nasty little pipsqueak, only interested in yourself."

Boss Beak blinked, then his eyes widened as he recognized the eccentric explorer he remembered from his boyhood. "Shackleton Flipper?"

he gasped. "You're alive?"

Shackleton surveyed the melting buildings, the black cloud of pollution and the slush lapping round his feet. His low voice rose against Boss Beak. "I remember when I departed this place all those many years ago, the sky sang with birds and the sea teemed with fish. The snow was crisp under a penguin's feet. The air was clean and cold in his beak. A penguin lived in what he could, with certainty, call the most beautiful land upon this Earth." Then his voice rose angrily. "But you've ruined it, Beak. You've ruined it, you stupid selfish money-grabbing fool!"

"Now you listen to me—" roared Boss Beak, jabbing Shackleton's breast with his flipper.

Dude stepped between them. "Lay off him, man."

Boss Beak squealed to the crowd, "This muscle-bound idiot has just assaulted me! You all saw!" He turned to Dude. "I'll have you thrown in prison. See how 'cool' you are doing five years' bird in Penguinville Prison—"

Dude grabbed Boss Beak by the scruff of the neck and hoisted him high into the air. His legs flailed as he tried to wriggle free, but Dude held him in a vice-like grip.

The crowd cheered.

Scott shouted, "Down with Beak! Down

with Beak!"

Soon every penguin was joining in. "DOWN WITH BEAK! DOWN WITH BEAK! DOWN WITH BEAK!" they cried.

Boss Beak squawked, "I run this town and I command—"

Scott scooped up a slushy snowball and flung it straight at his enormous beak.

Within moments of being struck by the first one, Boss Beak was being plastered by snowballs from all angles, while the crowd carried on chanting, "DOWN WITH BEAK! DOWN WITH BEAK! DOWN WITH BEAK!"

Shackleton waved his flippers and the townspenguins fell silent. "We bring great news," he announced. "Penguins *can* reach the South Pole. There they can once again live in the most beautiful land on earth. And it's all thanks to these youngsters."

The crowd cheered.

Lots more girls gathered round Dude, feeling his muscles and giggling.

"Somehow, I think he'll get over me pretty quickly," Amelia whispered to Scott.

"You know, Amelia," Scott said, "this is only the beginning. There's a lot more work to do, if we're going to build a new Penguinville."

"I like that name. 'New Penguinville.' What d'you think it'll be like?"

"Cold," he said. "A hundred degrees below freezing – and that's in the height of summer."

"Lovely," she said. "And there'll be a big sign on the edge of town: WELCOME TO THE SOUTH POLE – NEW PENGUINVILLE IS PROUD TO BE POLLUTION FREE. It'll be the most beautiful land on Earth, and it'll stay that way for ever."

"You make it sound like it already exists," he said.

"I don't think it'll be too long before it does," she said.

"Neither do I," he said.